COUNTRY COUSIN

COUNTRY COUSIN

Elizabeth Hawksley

Chivers Press • Thorndike Press
Bath, Avon, England • Thorndike, Maine USA

This Large Print edition is published by Chivers Press, England
and by Thorndike Press, USA.

Published in 1996 in the U.K. by arrangement with Robert Hale Limited.

Published in 1996 in the U.S. by arrangement with John Johnson Ltd.

U.K. Hardcover ISBN 0–7451–4906–5 (Chivers Large Print)
U.K. Softcover   ISBN 0–7451–4918–9 (Camden Large Print)
U.S. Softcover   ISBN 0–7862–0713–2 (General Series Edition)

The text of this Large Print edition is unabridged.
Other aspects of the book may vary from the original edition.

Set in 16 pt. New Times Roman.

Printed in Great Britain on acid-free paper.

British Library Cataloguing in Publication Data available

Library of Congress Cataloging-in-Publication Data

Hawksley, Elizabeth.
  Country cousin / Elizabeth Hawksley.
    p.   cm.
  ISBN 0–7862–0713–2 (lg. print : sc)
  1. Large type books.   I. Title.
[PR6058.A8965C6   1996]
823'.914–dc20
                                                                    96–12864

To my dear aunt, Maggie Cook,
with much love

CHAPTER ONE

The phaeton swerved between the barrow boy and the pavement with inches to spare. There was a muffled shriek from a young lady who had been about to cross the road, and a volley of less genteel curses from the barrow boy as his load of oranges cascaded on to the cobblestones. The driver of the phaeton halted, jumped down, directed his tiger towards the barrow boy and went to the assistance of the lady.

The lady who was standing on the pavement, angrily stamping her foot, could scarcely be more than seventeen years of age, thought the gentleman. Deucedly pretty, and not just in the common style, with auburn curls and bright sea-green eyes in a piquante little face. She wore the demure but expensive dress of a debutante, with a green promenade pelisse of gros de Naples and a charming poke bonnet in pale-green straw underneath which her curls danced. She had something of the look of a pretty little kitten, thought the gentleman, and probably as wilful.

'You have made me drop my bandboxes, sir!'

'And you, miss, were not looking where you were going,' retorted the gentleman with infuriating calm. 'Come now, your parcels have taken no hurt. But surely you are not alone here? Where is your maid? Or have you perhaps,' he added teasingly, 'run away from the schoolroom?'

'Schoolroom!' The lady pulled herself up to her full five foot one and a half inches. 'I am *seventeen*, sir. I shall be making my come-out this spring. Besides, my cousin is with me.' She gestured behind her to where a lady in black was just coming out of a shop.

'Araminta! Oh dear, *now* what have you done?' The voice was soft and musical and held a hint of laughter.

'My chaperone, sir,' said Araminta triumphantly, with the air of a magician pulling a rabbit out of a hat after a particularly nasty moment.

The lady thus indicated came towards them and put one restraining hand on Araminta's sleeve. The gentleman gave her only a cursory glance, writing her off as possibly a poor relation, certainly a dowd. But in this he did her a grave injustice.

Phyllida Gainford was twenty-five, and had been widowed for some two years. Under her black crêpe her figure was slim and elegant. She had hair of a deep russet and the pale skin that sometimes accompanies such hair. Her eyes were green, like her cousin's, but whereas Araminta's were bright and vivid, Phyllida's were a deep green with hazel flecks and were her most expressive feature. Her face was a

2

lovely oval, but the black crêpe that betokened her widowed state drained it of any colour and made her look quite washed out. Unless you noticed the intelligence in those deep-green eyes and the humour lurking at the corners of her mouth it would be easy to dismiss her.

Phyllida's gaze took in the gentleman in front of her. He was tall, topping little Araminta by a good foot and was quite disturbingly good-looking, with a crop of fair curly hair in careful dishevelment *à la Titus*, deep-blue eyes and a firm well-cut mouth, just now twitching slightly in amusement as he looked down at Araminta. He wore an olive-green overcoat with a roll collar, a buff striped valencia waistcoat and tight-fitting fawn pantaloons with black Hessian half-boots. Phyllida did not need to glimpse the crest on the door of his phaeton to realize that this was a Corinthian of the first stare.

She was conscious of a tug of attraction that was instantly dismissed. There was something in that air of disdainful boredom with the world, that insufferable superiority over lesser mortals, that reminded her most painfully of her husband, Ambrose. Such a man would not hesitate to ride roughshod over anybody who got in his way, however magnetic his outward charm—and Phyllida ruefully acknowledged he had plenty of *that*! The task of chaperoning her young cousin was going to prove quite as difficult as she had feared. Araminta, wayward, spoilt and as pretty as a picture (not to mention her splendid dowry) was obviously set to be one of the belles of the Season. The gentleman in front of her was only the first of her many admirers.

How on earth was she, Phyllida, going to cope? She had lived all her life in a rural backwater in Gloucestershire, apart from her brief marriage. She was not used to Society. It was all very well for Grandmama to say that at twenty-five she was quite old enough to chaperone Araminta, but Phyllida knew herself to be shy and awkward in company, especially when the company in question was far more good-looking than any man had a right to be.

Phyllida's sense of humour came to her rescue. You may be as handsome as Adonis, she thought crossly, but you are also quite abominably rude staring at me in that disdainful way! She did not, most decidedly, value the man in front of her at his own valuation!

'Araminta,' she said firmly, 'do you know this gentleman?'

'No, I don't! And I am not at all sure I want to! He's rude and overbearing and drives too fast. He has the temerity to think that I am a schoolgirl. It's all the fault of this horrid dull pelisse!'

'Try for a little civility, please, Araminta.'

'I *told* Grandmama,' went on Araminta

4

unheeding. 'If you are my height you need something more, well, startling. Otherwise you get overlooked.'

The gentleman looked amused. 'I cannot imagine anybody overlooking you, Miss ... er?'

'Stukeley,' said Araminta, 'and this is my cousin, Mrs Gainford.'

'Gainford? Not one of the Avenell Gainfords?'

'I am Captain Ambrose Gainford's widow, sir.'

'Ah yes.' The gentleman frowned, but said nothing further.

Phyllida looked at him with a sudden unease. Her husband had been killed at Waterloo after only three months of marriage, and although that melancholy event was now nearly two years ago, some polite condolences might have been in order. But not only was this tall, arrogant-looking gentleman saying nothing, his mouth was closed firmly on what he had been going to say.

'Did you know my husband?' she ventured.

'No.'

'Well,' said Araminta crossly, looking from one to the other. She was young and pretty enough to resent any attention wandering from herself. 'We have introduced ourselves. Pray, who are you?'

'FitzIvor,' said the gentleman shortly. 'Lord Hereward FitzIvor.'

5

Good heavens, thought Phyllida, so this is Lord Hereward FitzIvor. What was it Grandmama had said only yesterday evening? Corinthian *par excellence*, notable amateur in Jackson's Boxing Saloon, one of the best whips of the day and catch of the Season for the last eight or ten years. He was the younger brother of the Earl of Gifford, but quite as wealthy in his own right, for he had inherited his mother's fortune as well as her looks.

Little did Lord Hereward know it, but he was high on Grandmama's list of suitable husbands for Araminta.

*   *   *

'Well!' declared Araminta mischievously, when she and Phyllida were seated in their carriage later. 'I declare I am quite nuts on Lord Hereward already, are not you, Phyl?'

Phyllida reflected that his manners had not led him to offer to carry the bandboxes, and that while Araminta had been treated with all gentlemanly courtesy, *she* had been left walking behind carrying a number of unwieldy parcels. But then, such a beau would hardly demean himself by carrying parcels in a public place. She giggled suddenly, picturing this elegant creature staggering under a tower of hatboxes: her sense of humour coming to the rescue of her outraged dignity.

'What is it?' asked Araminta.

'Nothing. Too foolish a thought to repeat.

6

But yes, Lord Hereward is very good-looking, I grant you. But I do not care for him myself.'

'But he is so very handsome!' cried Araminta, with all the artlessness of seventeen.

'Handsome is as handsome does,' retorted Phyllida, and tried to banish those amused blue eyes from her mind.

'He behaved very handsomely to me! Do you think he will call, as he said, Phyl? Whatever will Grandmama say?'

The Honourable Mrs Osborne, Phyllida's and Araminta's grandmother, was a lady whom her contemporaries both feared and disliked in equal measure. She was extremely wealthy, of strong opinions and quite unscrupulous in achieving her own ends. She was one of those dominating characters who tend to collect round themselves weaker-minded acolytes. One of these was Lady Albinia Marchmont, lady-in-waiting to old Queen Charlotte, another was the wife of General Sir Marmaduke Vavasour of the War Office, yet another an intimate of Lady Jersey's, patroness of Almack's. It was considered most unwise to be out of favour with Mrs Osborne, who had such strings to her bow, and never hesitated to use them.

Mrs Osborne had two surviving grandchildren, Araminta Stukeley and Phyllida Gainford. Araminta was the apple of her eye, indeed she had brought her up ever since the untimely deaths of Araminta's parents in a coach accident in Italy when Araminta was six. It was generally believed that Araminta would be her grandmother's sole heiress.

Phyllida's mother, Mrs Osborne's younger daughter, had married beneath her, a country squire of neither fortune nor ambition. Mr Herbert Danby had, however, a gentleness of temper and a sweetness of disposition that had appealed to the young Miss Anne Osborne. No arguments her mother could put forward, and they were many, had the power to sway her. Mrs Osborne was resolute in refusing her consent, and on the morning of her twenty-first birthday, Anne Osborne, with a small valise and accompanied by her maid, took the mail coach to Gloucester and married her Herbert there three weeks later.

They were extremely happy for ten years, until the beginnings of consumption struck, and the long-drawn agony of a fatal illness drew Anne and Herbert and little Phyllida into a self-imposed isolation. Anne had died when Phyllida was nineteen. It was Phyllida who coped with the sale of Danby Grange and the removal to a smaller house, for neglect and doctors' bills had long since ruined the small property. Her father, exhausted and broken-hearted, had retreated into the life of a recluse, seeing those old friends whose goodwill led them to call on him, but initiating no social contacts himself. Phyllida felt that in the circumstances she could do nothing other than refuse her almost unknown grandmother's offer of a London Season.

Mrs Osborne had been outraged by the refusal and, after a series of angry letters, had washed her hands of Phyllida. She relented so far as to send Phyllida a £50 bill every Christmas, 'From your affectionate grandmother, Cecilia Osborne', but apart from that she appeared to have vanished from their lives.

Phyllida was not blind to her father's shortcomings. While her mother was alive he could be happy and social, and as a child Phyllida had fitted into her parents' doings happily enough. When her mother died the mainspring of his life broke and he seemed to have no energy for anything. It was Phyllida who organized his affairs, ran his household with sympathetic efficiency and took his problems on her young shoulders. She grew up to be quiet and a little shy in company, but with an inner strength and the saving grace of a sense of humour that only those close to her ever discovered.

It was not until she was twenty-two that Phyllida allowed herself to be persuaded to leave home. Her godmother, Mrs Cade, invited her to Brighton for a month. Surely Herbert would allow his daughter a small holiday? It would be very quiet, for it was February, and there was no Society worth speaking of in Brighton until the summer months, wrote Mrs Cade.

But Mrs Cade's quiet was not the quiet of a Gloucestershire village. The –nth Regiment was stationed near and Mrs Cade was social. Phyllida met Captain Ambrose Gainford, newly returned with his regiment from America. Amid the whirl of life in Brighton with its parties and assemblies, Phyllida fell desperately in love. Her emotions, so long saddened and chastened, burst into life. She and Ambrose were married in the March of 1815, just before his regiment was ordered to Belgium. Phyllida and Mrs Cade accompanied him.

When Phyllida wrote to inform her grandmother of her marriage, Mrs Osborne's reaction was instantaneous: Ambrose Gainford was untrustworthy, a libertine and a gambler. If he or Phyllida thought that they could lay their hands on one penny of her money then they were very much mistaken. She had no doubt at all that he would run through what little money Phyllida had before many months were out and then she would regret her foolish and impetuous marriage. She, Cecilia Osborne, declined to take any further interest in her granddaughter.

Those three months in Belgium passed in a feverish round of pleasure and growing anxiety. Phyllida now could hardly recall the separate incidents, the picnics, the balls, the military comings and goings. All the time there were the rumours, each day stronger and more frightening, of Napoleon's imminent arrival, culminating in those last three days of battle— the distant rumble of cannon, carts full of fleeing refugees, the arrival of the wounded and, finally, after a day or two of dwindling hope, the dead. Ambrose was killed at Waterloo on the eighteenth of June, 1815.

Phyllida had retreated home broken and exhausted, vowing never to leave it again. Her life was over. Ambrose was dead. What else was there for her?

It was not until early in 1817 that she heard again from her grandmother.

My dear Phyllida, Mrs Osborne wrote, and continued with ominous condescension:

I have decided to overlook your Undutiful Behaviour on the occasion of your Unhappy Marriage: you did not have the Benefit of my Advice. You may, therefore, count yourself once again, a granddaughter of mine, and thus be eligible for the Advantages I have in store for you.

The Almighty has seen fit to plague me with arthritis and I find myself unable to chaperone my other granddaughter, your cousin Araminta, during her Season. You, however, as a widow of some years standing, and past the age of Foolish Behaviour I trust, may do so. I shall, of course, pay all your expenses and

11

am determined to Settle a suitable sum on you: ten thousand pounds if you marry while I am alive, or an annuity of five hundred a year after I am gone.

I shall require you to come to Town by the beginning of March at the latest, for your wardrobe must be thought of and I shall want to instruct you how you must go on.

My respects to your Papa, and I trust he has the Sense to put your welfare first on this Occasion.

Your affectionate grandmother,
Cecilia Osborne

Phyllida did not know whether to be outraged by her grandmother's calm determination to organize her life, or amused by her poor regard for the Deity in forcing such a solution upon her. She would refuse it, of course. She could not leave Papa a second time.

Her father thought otherwise. 'No, my dear little Phyl,' he said firmly. 'You must go. Pooh! What's three months or so to me? Molly will look after me well enough. Besides, Phyl, your grandmother is right. I have not considered your welfare as I ought.'

'Nonsense, dear Papa.'

'It is true, my dear. There is very little money when I am gone, you know. It would ease my mind considerably if I knew that you were adequately provided for. I think you should do as your grandmother wishes.'

12

Phyllida reluctantly agreed and some three weeks later found herself in London. She had expected that her position as Araminta's chaperone would be largely a sinecure, for, in spite of her complaints, it was obvious that Mrs Osborne enjoyed her frail health, and only allowed it to discommode her if there was something she did not wish to do. Araminta, with her looks and her expectations, was obviously going to be one of the Season's most successful débutantes. Mrs Osborne would not wish to miss her granddaughter's triumphs.

But something Araminta said in the carriage going home after their abrupt introduction to Lord Hereward, made Phyllida wonder whether, after all, her job was going to prove more wearing than she had counted on.

'You know, Phyl,' said Araminta, examining the tassels on her reticule, 'I do not think we should mention meeting Lord Hereward, after all.'

'Oh?'

'You see, I really do not like to be pushed. Grandmama somehow seems to be able to make people do what she wants, and if she thought that Lord Hereward was taken with me ... Of course, I should like to be married sometime, but I plan to have some fun first!'

'What kind of fun?' enquired Phyllida, her heart sinking.

'All sorts of fun. When I was at my seminary in Bath, Belinda Borrowdale and I slipped out one evening and went to the circus! Don't look so horrified, you timid thing! It was quite safe; we had some escorts. Not quite out of the top drawer, you might say,' Araminta giggled, 'but perfectly respectable, I assure you.'

'I trust that you returned home without being detected,' said Phyllida calmly.

'Lord, yes! Belinda had left the schoolroom window off the catch, so we simply climbed in.'

Phyllida reflected that while she herself was quieter and more retiring, Miss Stukeley was plainly made of sterner stuff! Araminta would inherit more from her grandmother than her fortune: she had inherited her determination to go her own way. Phyllida tried not to think what would happen if she should ever be caught between those two strong wills. She could only cross her fingers and hope that the gaieties of the Season would suffice to put all thoughts of incognito excursions out of her cousin's head.

*   *   *

Emma Winter, innkeeper's daughter, sometime actress and current mistress of Lord Hereward FitzIvor, sat at her marble-topped dressing-table and coaxed a blue-black ringlet to lie prettily on her slender neck. She smiled at her reflection in the glass. What was it he had called her? Aphrodite? Well, it was true! She *was* beautiful. And if her grey eyes were as hard

14

as granite and those pretty lips a little mean, those were faults most gentlemen were easily able to brush aside.

Ever since that foolish episode with that handsome young soldier when she was sixteen, Emma had been able to twist men around her little finger. She deserved every penny of the luxury Hereward kept her in: she never permitted any irritation to annoy him, she was cleverer than that! There were other ways of getting what she wanted after all. She knew how to dress well without being vulgar and, most important, she had a full and voluptuous body which she knew how to use.

There was a scratch at her door and Polly, her maid, entered. 'Lord Hereward is here, madam.'

'Thank you, Polly. I shall be with him in ten minutes. Tell James to bring his Lordship the sherry, will you?'

'Certainly, miss.'

When she entered her drawing-room some ten minutes later, Lord Hereward was looking far from loverlike.

'Well, Emma, and what were you doing at the theatre, last night?'

'The ... the theatre?'

'Yes, the Olympic. I thought I had made my views perfectly clear.'

How the devil had he known about that, thought Emma. She had gone heavily cloaked—even taken a hackney rather than

15

her own carriage. 'Oh, darling! What a frown! It was all perfectly innocuous, I assure you. Poor old Tom Cooper's benefit night. Of course, his dancing is not what it was, but he was so kind to me in the old days, that when his wife sent a message *begging* me to support him, what could I do?'

'You could have said no and sent him a guinea.'

'And hurt one of my oldest friends?'

'I have never heard of this "oldest friend" before.'

'But darling.' Emma opened her eyes wide. 'You have always said that you do not want to hear about my acting days. Otherwise, of course, I should have told you about dear Tom.'

Hereward looked at her sceptically, but said nothing. Emma moved across the room, every line of her body visible through her dampened petticoat. She allowed her silver gauze shawl to slip, revealing one white shoulder and the outline of her full breast.

Treacherous bitch, thought Hereward, watching her through narrowed eyes. He jerked his head towards the door. 'Lock it!'

'Here?' Emma raised her eyebrows, glancing over her shoulder at the sofa.

'Why not?' Hereward tugged at his cravat.

Some time later Emma lazily moved an arm and reached for her petticoat. Hereward sat up and retrieved his shirt from the floor. 'I'll be back tonight,' he promised. 'This afternoon I promised my grandmother I'd pay a call with her.'

'A call?' Emma frowned. 'This is very unlike you, darling. No doubt,' she added sullenly, 'the object of your "call" is very beautiful.'

'I've no notion of tying myself up with any female, as well you know,' replied Hereward shortly. 'This is a courtesy call only. Grandmama wishes to visit an old friend, a Mrs Osborne, and her two granddaughters. One, Miss Stukeley, is a mere schoolroom miss, the other, a Mrs Gainford, a somewhat dowdy widow. I hope you are satisfied.'

'Gainford,' repeated Emma slowly. 'I used to know a Gainford some years ago.'

'There must be many Gainfords,' said Hereward impatiently. 'This widow married one of the Avenell Gainfords—killed at Waterloo, I believe.'

Emma shrugged and then laughed. 'Enjoy yourself,' she said. 'I expect you'll be thoroughly bored with schoolgirl chat and widows' reminiscences, so I shall hope to find you very appreciative of my efforts to amuse you this evening!'

'I shall be!'

When he had gone, Emma turned to stare out of the window, her eyes suddenly steely. Gainford, she thought, could it be *Ambrose* he was talking about? God forbid Hereward had met Ambrose's widow!

17

The Dowager Countess of Gifford, a strikingly handsome old lady with bright blue eyes and carefully curled white hair, sat in the Blue Saloon at Gifford House, St James's Square, and looked at her grandsons over the tea table with affectionate exasperation. Hereward was twenty-eight now and Thorold over thirty and where were her flock of little grandchildren? It was too bad that her declining years were spent worrying about the succession and bullying her reluctant grandsons into some notion of their family responsibilities. And in neither case could she deceive herself that her success had been more than minimal.

Thorold, her elder grandson, now Earl of Gifford, was practically a hermit: whatever could be done about him? It was too bad that his wife, Drusilla, had died in childbed. The Dowager had done what she could, she had dragged the Earl up to London every Season since he was eighteen. Thorold was a good-natured young man and obligingly went along with his grandmother's fiction that at her age she needed him as an escort, but nobody seeing her hobnobbing with her friends or playing cards with tireless energy into the small hours could possibly believe in her decrepitude.

If the Earl did not attend all the balls and parties his grandmother would have liked, at least he escorted her a respectable number of times to Almack's, and appeared at her own parties and soirées with a good grace. Admittedly, he also spent time with a number of antiquarian bookseller friends of his or pursued various elusive scholarly references with his friend Sir John Soane, none of which could conceivably be supposed to further any matrimonial plans.

What on earth was the matter with the man, thought her ladyship. His father had been lively enough, in fact there had been several episodes with opera dancers and one more serious one with a bogus comtesse fleeing from the French Revolution that even now she didn't like to think about, but Thorold seemed largely impervious to feminine charm. It was not as if he was bad-looking or unintelligent. He didn't have the Grecian profile of his brother, but he was a tall, well-made man with thick brown wavy hair and warm brown eyes. He was kind and affectionate, so why didn't he settle down and secure the succession?

It was then that she thought back to Drusilla. Two years ago Thorold had startled her by marrying Drusilla Shotton. She was the daughter of the vicar down at Maynard, a nobody, but it was done before she had gathered her wits about her to protest. Nobody knew what Thorold had seen in Drusilla, who was so colourless that Lady Gifford had difficulty in remembering what she looked like. She had had no conversation beyond 'yes' and

19

'no' and occasionally, 'quite so'.

In disgust Lady Gifford had moved to the Dower House, only to return some ten months later when Drusilla died in childbirth, leaving the Earl with a baby daughter. Lady Caroline FitzIvor was now a toddler whose energy and liveliness had her nurserymaid running after her from dawn to dusk. But she was the wrong sex, and Thorold must remarry. Lady Gifford did not grudge Thorold his daughter, but felt that it was typical of the late countess to die in that indeterminate way, leaving the most important thing undone.

But if Thorold was set in his ways, then Hereward must marry. There was no question of *him* not appreciating the female sex, if gossip was to be believed. He had started in the petticoat line at Oxford and stories of barques of frailty he had taken under his protection were legion. The latest one, La Winter, so she heard, ran true to form: voluptuous, beautiful and rapacious. Well, he could afford it, more was the pity, and how could the immature charms of some girl of birth and fortune tempt a man who had Emma Winter in keeping?

Still, she would not despair. He had obviously enjoyed his unconventional meeting with little Araminta Stukeley, let that be a start. Perhaps even Thorold might find the quiet Mrs Gainford to his taste, not that she wished for a connection with that ramshackle family, but it might at least encourage Thorold

20

to look about him a little.

The day of Mrs Osborne's At Home, that lady's drawing-room contained two people whom she could well have done without in view of the fact that she was expecting the Countess of Gifford and her grandsons to call. One was Lady Selina Lemmon, one-time friend of the Princess of Wales and now, since Caroline's eclipse, treading a precarious line between obscurity and being tolerated for her knowledge of the latest scandals. Nothing, Mrs Osborne thought crossly, would be more likely to make Lord Hereward shy off than Lady Selina's busy eyes and inquisitive tongue.

The other was her dashing but impecunious godson, Antony Herriot. It was a pity that convention did not allow her to forbid him the house. It had been all right while Araminta was still in the schoolroom and Antony a scrubby schoolboy, but he had turned out far too handsome, considering his lack of prospects. He must be discouraged from a closer acquaintance with her impressionable granddaughter.

Mr Herriot thought otherwise, for he had long ago spent his small patrimony and now relied on his charm, his fair good looks, and the uncertain fortunes of the gaming table.

Mrs Osborne did her best to separate them by placing Antony firmly in a corner between Lady Selina and Phyllida. Lady Selina had glanced once at Phyllida and written her off as a dowd. She turned her attention to Antony.

'My dear Lady Selina.' Antony took her fingers and kissed them lightly. 'Now, do tell me, is what I hear about the Creditons true?'

'Well, they do say,' replied Lady Selina, her eyes sparkling with malice, 'that since a certain Captain S appeared, the lady has been finding some consolation.'

'No!'

'Of course, Mr C is looking the other way. He had his own amusements after all. But what is so diverting is...'

'*Who* says, Lady Selina,' put in Phyllida quietly, her hands clasped in her lap to hide their angry trembling. She had met Mrs Crediton recently and had learned that she had just lost a child. It seemed to her quite disgusting that her name should be bandied about in such a fashion.

Lady Selina laughed uncertainly, two spots of angry colour flying in her cheeks. 'Oh, I must protect my sources!' Why, the preachy little madam—she needed a set-down. Nobody spoke in that fashion to her!

Damned interfering prig, thought Antony. He'd have to see that she did not put a spoke in his wheel with little Araminta. The awkward pause which followed was broken by the arrival of the Countess of Gifford and her grandsons. Antony leaped to his feet and somehow when they were all sat down again, it was not Lord Hereward who was sitting on the

22

sofa next to Araminta as Mrs Osborne had hoped, but Antony. Lord Hereward, looking resigned, was sitting next to Phyllida, and Thorold was manfully listening to Lady Selina, a task he found difficult as he had no idea to whom her sets of coy initials referred.

'I know I should not be sitting here,' whispered Antony to Araminta, 'but Mrs Gainford terrifies me.'

'Phyllida? No! Why?'

'She looks so very starchy and respectable. I am sure she means to chaperone you very closely.'

Araminta looked across the room at Phyllida who sat, her head inclined at a stiff angle as she talked to Lord Hereward. She was at the age where her opinions of people veered wildly and instantly her cousin changed from being rather quiet but nice, to being a regular gaoler. Antony read her emotions easily enough on her expressive little face, and was satisfied.

'Why should you not be sitting here?' enquired Araminta next. 'You are Grandmama's godson.'

'True. But I am the black sheep of the family, you must know. I am surprised that Godmama has not warned you against me already.'

'Oh, I shan't regard it, I assure you. Why, you brought me some peppermint creams when I had chicken pox!'

'Lady Selina will tell you that I am not to

be trusted.'

'Pooh, who cares for her, the malicious creature. I choose my own friends!'

'My dear, they are both right.' Antony put on his sincere and noble look for a moment. 'They will say that I have been reckless and extravagant, and it is true. Sweet Araminta, if only I had known ... but what is the use?'

'But Antony...'

'No, no more.' Antony smiled at her ruefully and allowed Lady Gifford on Araminta's other side to take over the conversation. The seeds were sown. He could afford to wait. When his object was Araminta's £60,000, Antony had an inexhaustible supply of patience.

Lord Hereward stifled a yawn and wished himself back with Emma, indulging in some afternoon amorous dalliance. He had every intention of pursuing his acquaintance with Araminta a little, if only to amuse himself. But he had no intention of jockeying for position with Antony Herriot, especially under Lady Selina Lemmon's interested eye. He turned to Phyllida, who was sitting next to him.

'How do you go on in London, Mrs Gainford?'

'I like it very well, my lord.' Why was she feeling suddenly breathless? Phyllida wasn't sure she even *liked* the man!

'Really?' Hereward looked bored. 'Are there no drawbacks? Somehow I always understood that country folk found the pace of life here too fast and felt quite left behind.'

Phyllida flushed. Could this rudeness be deliberate? 'Are you suggesting that because I live in the country therefore I must be a clodhopper, my lord?'

Hereward frowned, he was not at all used to being taken up on his idle remarks. He knew, quite as well as Phyllida did that he was being unpardonably rude, but any woman who was attached to Ambrose Gainford deserved everything she got. He looked over her black crêpe dress disdainfully. 'And are you?' he enquired.

'I am sure that you are perfectly capable of deciding that for yourself, without succumbing to mere popular prejudice in the matter,' retorted Phyllida, suppressing a surge of exhilaration.

Hereward looked at her again. So she was not such a dull mouse after all. Her skin was good, her eyes most unusual and, if she discarded that abominable widow's cap and came out of her blacks, she might be quite passable. All the same, he could not forget poor Johnny, who had trusted Ambrose and had died, disgraced, because of it. He shut his eyes quickly to get rid of the image of that stairwell and the swinging body. Did she not *care* for what had happened that she should come to London? Well, Mrs Osborne and his grandmother plainly considered it of no account and doubtless Society would follow, but nobody who had been a friend of Johnny's could ever forget.

'I was surprised not to see you at your mama-in-law's At Home, Mrs Gainford.'

'My ... my mama-in-law, did you say?'

Hereward observed her white face with grim satisfaction and continued, 'You surely did not suppose your late husband to be motherless?' His tone implied that such a country bumpkin's ignorance would not surprise him.

'I ... I have never met Mrs Gainford.'

'Indeed?'

Phyllida glanced helplessly at Mrs Osborne. How could she explain that Ambrose had put off telling his parents of his marriage until it was too late? When she wrote after his death she had received the barest acknowledgement and an absolute refusal to continue the allowance hitherto paid to her husband. The marriage had not had their blessing, wrote Mrs Gainford icily. It had not occurred to Phyllida before how awkward a meeting with Ambrose's parents might prove to be; she had supposed them to be living quietly in Avenell.

'I—I am not acquainted with my mama-in-law,' stammered Phyllida. 'My ... my father was ill. And then the circumstances of Ambrose's death ... I had no time to do anything other than return home to look after Papa.'

Lord Hereward's silence was sceptical and

Phyllida felt herself grow hot. For some reason he disliked her. He plainly found her stumbling explanations unsatisfactory. It had never crossed her mind to question it before, but now she began to wonder why old Mrs Gainford had chosen not to acknowledge her, especially as ... She caught herself up, tears springing suddenly to her eyes. No, she must not think of that. Mrs Gainford now. Perhaps Lord Hereward was aware of some family secret that she did not know, but however could she ask him? The Gainfords were an old and respected family, but then so were the Danbys, her father's family, and her mother had been an Osborne. Ambrose, dearly though she had loved him, had been extravagant and unreliable, a charming wastrel. It would have been more natural for the Gainfords to have welcomed so respectable a daughter-in-law with open arms. Why *had* the Gainfords not acknowledged her as Ambrose's widow?

Lady Selina, her long nose quivering as if scenting scandal, was leaning forward towards them. Phyllida could only be grateful when Lady Gifford leaned forward to say, 'I understand that you come from Gloucestershire, Mrs Gainford. Whereabouts, may I ask?'

'I live near Cheltenham, Lady Gifford.'

'Cheltenham. Are you acquainted with the Melvilles?'

'My father knows Mr Arthur Melville very

27

well. They are both keen lepidopterists.'

Lady Gifford laughed. 'So like Arthur! Well, my dear, I have just been saying to your grandmother that you and Miss Stukeley must come with me to the opera.'

'Thank you, I should enjoy that.'

Hereward glanced at Araminta's appalled face and said, laughing, 'I am sure that Miss Stukeley would rather come riding in the park one morning. We are not all of us enamoured of Cimarosa's music.'

'Thank you, Lady Gifford,' said Araminta politely. 'And I should *love* to come riding, Lord Hereward.'

Hereward looked at Mrs Osborne. 'I shall take very good care of her, ma'am.'

Mrs Osborne demurred, 'I really do not think,' she began. 'Araminta is so reckless...'

Phyllida looked down at her hands. Lord Hereward had not asked her to go with them and plainly did not intend to. But Araminta could not go alone with him, he must know that.

Thorold leaned forward. 'May I make a suggestion,' he said mildly. 'Perhaps if Mrs Gainford and I were to accompany them, you might feel able to allow Miss Stukeley to go. People will tell you that I am a very dull fellow, Mrs Gainford, but you may always admire the flowers, you know.'

'I think you have a very kind heart, Lord Gifford,' said Phyllida gratefully, as Mrs

28

Osborne smiled and consented. And far better manners than your brother, she added to herself. 'I shall be very pleased to have your company.'

Thorold mopped his forehead thankfully. He'd managed that pretty well, he thought. Mrs Gainford looked far less alarming than Miss Stukeley, who looked the sort of girl who would expect him to flirt with her. One of the things he missed most about his wife was that her presence prevented all the other girls from making up to him. He always found it so awkward; he was never able to respond lightly to their teasing and half the time he couldn't understand it. He supposed he must be a veritable stick-in-the-mud. If Grandmama would but leave him alone to enjoy his books! If only Hereward would marry and secure the earldom. Or if Caroline ... no, he didn't want that. Caroline was perfect, just as she was, he wouldn't change her for all the heirs in the world.

Lady Gifford rose to her feet, and after due courtesies, left with her grandsons. As soon as they had departed Antony stood up to go. He didn't make the mistake of lingering over saying goodbye to Araminta. He flicked her carelessly on the cheek and said that he expected he would see her sometime. He politely expressed the hope that Phyllida would enjoy her visit and perhaps he could persuade her to stand up with him one evening

29

at Almack's? Mrs Osborne's expression relaxed. Thank God Antony was being sensible: she would send him £50 for his birthday. Of course, sooner or later he'd try to marry money—just so long as it was not Araminta's.

I shall have to tread warily, thought Antony. The meetings must be casual, not contrived. He would just have to put in an appearance at all those deuced rout parties and balls: he could see Lady Telford's invitation standing on their mantelpiece, his own invitation had arrived yesterday; he would accept it. It would be damned dull, but with the Osborne fortune at stake he grudged no exertion. He bowed politely to Phyllida, waved casually to Araminta and kissed Mrs Osborne's cheek. He was followed downstairs by Lady Selina.

'Dear Mr Herriot, may I take you up in my carriage?'

'I was going to White's, Lady Selina. It is only a step, thank you.'

'No, no, I insist. Look, it is coming on to rain.'

It wasn't, but Antony allowed himself to be persuaded. He stepped up into the carriage after her.

'Mr Herriot.' Lady Selina leaned towards him, almost overpowering him with her attar-of-roses. 'I scent a mystery, and you know how I love mysteries. That Mrs Gainford now, married one of the Avenell Gainfords, I gather.

30

Now *why* have the Gainfords kept so quiet about her, and why does Lord Hereward FitzIvor dislike her?'

'Does he?' Antony's eyes narrowed. 'But she has spent most of her life in Gloucestershire, I gather. I don't believe Lord Hereward has met her before.'

'Yet he was quite uncivil.'

'Hm. How very interesting.'

'Yes, isn't it. One longs to know more.'

Phyllida Gainford, thought Antony, was just the sort of interfering female who might become a damnable nuisance. It would be useful to have a way of ensuring her silence, if not her co-operation. Lady Selina was right, there *was* something not explained there; he couldn't put his finger on it yet, but he would, he would.

CHAPTER TWO

Phyllida sat up in bed, hugging her knees, and attempted to pull together her unruly thoughts. The whole visit was proving far more complicated than she had envisaged. Why had she not considered more carefully? She remembered, with a shudder, Mrs Gainford's icy politeness in reply to her letter after Ambrose's death. In some mysterious way Mrs Gainford managed to convey the impression that Phyllida was to blame if not for Ambrose's death precisely, then at least for the shocking way she had broken the news. Mrs Gainford's letter was edged in the deepest black and conveyed the impression that whereas a wife may have some sorrow, it was as nothing to the bereavement felt by his Parent.

Yet, Phyllida knew, for Ambrose had told her, that his family had more or less cut him off, and his mother never saw him but to lament over his shortcomings. Now, most awkwardly, Mrs Gainford was in Town.

Well, there was no use repining over an unjust fate. She must talk to her grandmother. After breakfast, in some trepidation, she knocked on the door of Mrs Osborne's bedroom—for her grandmother had her breakfast in bed on a tray and did all her correspondence from a small davenport in one corner of the room.

'Come in.'

Phyllida attempted to convey to her grandmother some of the awkwardness she felt on learning that Mrs Gainford was in Town, but Mrs Osborne, who herself had strongly disapproved of Phyllida's marriage, could hardly be expected to understand Phyllida's feelings.

Mrs Osborne had no opinion of Mrs Gainford. 'A most foolish woman,' she said briskly. 'I cannot believe that she will be in Town for long. She only comes up to consult

Dr Croft about her "nervous palpitations". He will suggest a depressing diet of beef tea and arrowroot. She will regale her visitors with an exact account of her indisposition, drag that put-upon cousin of hers around the shops and return home perfectly happy with her ill health. I have no patience with Augusta Gainford.'

'But in the meantime,' said Phyllida, 'what do I do? Lord Hereward has already been wondering why I have not visited her.'

Mrs Osborne frowned. 'It is quite impossible that she should deliberately be ignoring any granddaughter of mine,' she pronounced at last. Phyllida's eyes danced, but she said nothing. 'It may be that she is unaware that you are here. The Season has hardly started, we are still in April, after all. I believe a notice in the *Morning Post* that you are staying here will have the desired effect. Mrs Gainford must call. She will hardly wish to offend *me*.'

Phyllida could not match Mrs Osborne's sublime confidence: not even to her grandmother could she tell the most painful part of that letter. It was not only a question of whether Mrs Gainford would acknowledge her, but whether she, Phyllida, ever wished to see her at all. Not after ... she shook her head quickly and blinked away the threatening tears. She wished she had never agreed to come and longed, most passionately, for the peace and quiet of their Gloucestershire home and the undemanding society of her Papa.

Mrs Osborne dismissed her granddaughter and Phyllida went down to the morning-room she shared with Araminta. Araminta threw aside the embroidery as Phyllida entered and cried, 'Oh, good, here you are!' She patted the sofa beside her invitingly.

Phyllida pulled herself together and smiled. 'Well?' she said. 'What is it?'

'What is it?' squeaked Araminta. 'Oh, come now, Phyl, surely you haven't forgotten our visitors yesterday?'

Phyllida allowed herself to be beguiled into listening to Araminta's account of the call, Lord Gifford's shyness, but 'Something very kind about him, don't you think, Phyl?', Lord Hereward's classic good looks, and how he had looked at Araminta in such a way as made her quite embarrassed!

'And Mr Herriot?' asked Phyllida idly. She had not liked Mr Herriot, finding his interest in Lady Selina's gossip unpleasant, and his eyes as he looked at Araminta frankly calculating. Foolishly she said something deprecating to Araminta who flared up at once.

'I know he has been a rake, for he told me so himself!' So there! was implicit in her voice.

Phyllida realized that she had underestimated Mr Herriot and replied mildly, 'A lot of young men are, I believe. You are right to reprove me, for I have but met him the once. I expect I was swayed by him appearing to be on intimate terms with Lady Selina.'

'A horrid woman,' Araminta agreed, mollified, 'but An ... Mr Herriot says that he is only polite to her because of what she might say about him if he wasn't!'

Phyllida noticed the slip, but did not remark on it. Whatever Mr Herriot's attentions might be, he would, at least for the moment, be bound by the rules of Society. He might meet Araminta at dances, or ride with her in the Park, but he would not attempt anything of a clandestine nature: not if he was hoping to marry Araminta. She was only seventeen and Mr Herriot must know Mrs Osborne's uncertain temper. She had thrown over one granddaughter for an improvident marriage, she might well, if provoked, repudiate the other.

Should she hint as much to him? Better, at any rate, than voicing her fears to Mrs Osborne, whose reaction was likely to be both autocratic and immediate. Subtlety was quite unknown to her. But Araminta had too much of her grandmother in her to tolerate such a heavy-handed approach. No, it would have to be she, Phyllida, who did something. She sighed; it was not going to be the easy task to chaperone Araminta that Mrs Osborne had so confidently predicted.

But there was very little time for her to think about it. Mrs Osborne's mind had obviously been busy, for she summoned Phyllida once more to her bedroom and directed her to help with the invitations to the ball she was giving for Araminta. Phyllida also at her dictation, wrote to the *Morning Post* announcing her own arrival in the metropolis as the guest of her grandmother, the Hon. Mrs Osborne.

To Phyllida's alarm, Mrs Osborne did not stop there. In the afternoon she took her to her modiste in Bruton Street and ordered her a complete wardrobe suitable for a widow of impeccable standing who might now, apart perhaps from a faint nuance of grey or mauve, be considered out of mourning.

'But Grandmama,' expostulated Phyllida, feeling quite uncomfortably exposed and dowdy in that mirror-hung room with dozens of the most expensive fashion plates on a small table in front of her. 'I would not feel right … how can I possibly wear so many … something darker perhaps. …'

'Nonsense, Phyllida!' Mrs Osborne had had a quiet think in her room that morning and had waxed silently indignant at Mrs Gainford daring to disapprove of any granddaughter of hers! It was an aspect that had not occurred to her before, but now it had, she was determined that Phyllida should be seen to move in the highest circles and be quite independent of Mrs Gainford's approval. 'Now do not be tiresome, I pray. You will need several day dresses, a couple of walking dresses. Black? Certainly not! A most depressing colour for the young. Then you will need afternoon dresses and evening gowns, and then, of course a shawl, a pelisse, oh yes, a riding habit—that must be a priority, Miss Lannes.'

'*Oui, madame.*'

'But I have a pelisse, Grandmama!'

'Yes, and very shabby it is. It must be quite five years out of date! Fortunately, now you may wear colours again...'

'No! Grandmama, I could not!'

'Why not, pray? Is not two years long enough for that good-for-nothing?'

'You promised me that I should have to do nothing but chaperone Araminta,' begged Phyllida desperately. 'If I wear colours it will look as though I am on the catch myself.'

Mrs Osborne looked at Phyllida sternly. She had every intention of getting Phyllida married off as well—and this time under her eye, where she could see that the young man was a suitable *parti*. But, plainly, to suggest such a thing to Phyllida in her present state was out of the question. Much as she disliked being contradicted, she disliked any prospect of her longer-term plans being thwarted even more.

'Now, do not be thinking, Phyllida, that I have any idea of dressing you up as an *ingénue*. You are a married woman now, after all. I am not suggesting girlish pinks and blues for you, but perhaps a dark green for your riding habit? Or this discreet blue and white floral print for a morning dress? Nothing could be more elegant.

37

'As for re-marriage, my dear, calm yourself. My concern is with Araminta, and if while she is coming-out you make a few agreeable friends yourself, you do not object to that, surely? You know, Phyllida, you are now five-and-twenty. Most young men are looking for birth, beauty and a large portion: they may be as choosy as they please.'

'Of course, ma'am, you are right,' said Phyllida, brightening up.

But no girl could be quite depressed after a day's shopping to her heart's content and Phyllida was no exception. She had already realized that her dowdy black clothes, far from making her inconspicuous, made her the subject of a lot of unpleasant enquiries. Maybe Grandmama was right: to wear colours again and fashionable dresses would make her more unremarkable amid so many pretty (and well-endowed) girls.

* * *

Phyllida's mama-in-law, Mrs Gainford, sat in her boudoir gently sipping her morning chocolate and tried to decide whether a visit to her favourite milliner or a gentle stroll down the new Burlington Arcade would most benefit her health, when a paragraph in the *Morning Post* caught her eye. She uttered a shriek, which brought her companion and cousin into the room.

'My dear cousin,' panted Amelia, her iron curls still bobbing wildly from her haste. 'Whatever is it?'

'Look! Look at *that*, Amelia.' Mrs Gainford pointed with an accusing finger at the offending paragraph. '... *and Mrs Ambrose Gainford is residing with her grandmother, the Honourable Mrs Osborne for the Season.*'

'Is that Ambrose's...' stammered Amelia.

'Yes,' cried Mrs Gainford. 'Whatever am I to do, Amelia?'

'Does ... does she know?'

'Of course not. I hoped never to hear from her again. She seemed quite satisfactorily stuck in that Gloucestershire retreat of hers. I was quite certain that Mrs Osborne had repudiated her; in fact, I made the most careful enquiries. There seemed not the slightest danger of ever encountering her again, so I thought...'

'Oh, how awkward.' Amelia clasped her hands together. 'What shall you do?'

Mrs Gainford pushed her cup and saucer away impatiently. 'I shall have to see her, of course. Oh, *why* must she come now, just when I have persuaded Mr Gainford that I would be better for a month or so in Town.'

Amelia understood her. Mr Gainford, a man known for his parsimony, only with the greatest reluctance allowed his wife to come to London, and then only if one of her relations put her up and spared him the cost of lodgings or hotel bills. This year, the first time for several years, an old school-friend, travelling on the Continent with her husband, had offered her house to Mrs Gainford for a few months.

Mrs Gainford began to cry, 'I can't go back to Avenell, not when I've just arrived. Oh, how cruel it is!'

'You ... you couldn't tell her ...' suggested her cousin.

'*Tell* her! Are you out of your mind, Amelia? What, pray, do you think Mrs Osborne would have to say?'

'She might send her home?'

'But what about *me*? She wouldn't stop there. Do you think she wouldn't make it impossible for me ever to come here again? No, it's not to be thought of!'

'And that actress?'

Mrs Gainford shuddered. 'Dreadful, dreadful female! But there's no reason why she should interfere—even if she hears of Mrs Ambrose's existence, which I doubt. She is probably still touring in second-rate theatres in the provinces somewhere. In any case, the settlement was final, Mr Gainford's lawyer made sure of that.'

'My dearest Augusta, then everything will be all right! Acknowledge Mrs Ambrose—you need do no more than that. *Your* uncertain health is well known. *She* has been looking after an invalid father. Who is to know that you have not been corresponding these last

40

two years?'

'Very true, Amelia.' Mrs Gainford brightened up. 'And ten to one, if she is reasonably pretty, which I have no doubt she is, or Ambrose would not have chosen her, she will find another husband and then the whole worry will have gone.'

'Re-marriage must be in Mrs Osborne's mind,' pointed out her cousin.

'So it must.' Mrs Gainford brightened up still more. 'Now I must dress, Amelia, and then you must help me compose a letter to Mrs Ambrose, requesting her to call.'

* * *

Hereward sat in front of his long shaving mirror while his valet shaved him and stared unseeing at his reflection. He could not get Phyllida out of his mind, try as he might to superimpose the image of Araminta's gamine prettiness, or even Emma's more obvious charms. He had been abominably uncivil to Phyllida, he knew it, and she had responded with a quiet dignity and then a flash of anger that quite startled him. Hereward was not used to feeling uncomfortable at his own behaviour, but he felt so now, and he didn't like it. Damn it, she was Gainford's widow—two of a kind— and doubtless still living off her ill-gotten gains. Johnny had dropped £10,000 that fatal night and it had been Gainford who had introduced him to that gaming hell.

'Please, my lord, keep still,' implored his valet, for Hereward had banged his fist on the chair arm involuntarily.

And yet, Hereward's thoughts resumed, she had not seemed that sort of woman, she had seemed, if anything, rather shy. Pretty too, or she would be out of that dreadful black, trim, with a pleasing figure and lovely eyes, not at all the sort of showy article Gainford usually favoured.

His valet gave his face a final wipe and surveyed him anxiously. Hereward nodded. The valet held out a red brocade smoking jacket and Hereward absently put it on.

'I shall want you later, John, I am engaged to go out riding.'

'Very good, my lord.'

In the breakfast parlour he found his brother waiting. He went to the sideboard and poured himself a cup of coffee, took a liberal helping of kidneys and bacon and sat down.

'Well, Thorold, are you ready for Mrs Gainford and Miss Stukeley this morning?'

'Yes,' said Thorold miserably, thinking how he would much prefer to potter off and discuss rare book bindings with his friend, Sir John Soane. But he had his duty to do. Grandmama had made it quite clear that he was to escort Mrs Gainford and leave Miss Stukeley to captivate Hereward.

'Most agreeable lady, Mrs Gainford,' he

42

said valiantly, 'I shall look forward to talking to her.'

Hereward looked at him sceptically and raised an enquiring eyebrow.

'All right!' Thorold laughed suddenly, a deep chuckle that had made more than one young lady wonder why he was not more forthcoming, since his laugh was so infectious. 'It's Grandmama, of course. I am to talk to Mrs Gainford...'

'And I am to be enchanted by the delicious Araminta,' finished Hereward. Between them the countess and Thorold had made everything easy for him. Why then did he feel so unaccountably put out?

* * *

Phyllida might have been expected to feel some awkwardness at the prospect of riding with Lord Hereward, even if she obeyed Mrs Osborne and saw that he conversed with her cousin as much as possible. But by the morning of their riding engagement another event had pushed any thoughts of Hereward's uncivility right out of her mind. For the previous day, the very day of the notice in the *Morning Post*, Phyllida had received a violet-scented letter from her mother-in-law.

'She asks me to go to tea this afternoon, Grandmama,' she said, as she and Mrs Osborne sat in the morning-room. Mrs

Osborne looked up from her embroidery.

'May I see?'

Phyllida handed her the letter. Mrs Osborne raised her lorgnette and surveyed the letter at arm's length. 'Hm, usual excuses ... must not exert herself ... compliments to me ... quiet tea and chat. You must go.'

'Yes,' Phyllida sighed.

'Danbury will bring the carriage round at four.'

Phyllida, dressed in one of her new afternoon dresses of lilac-spotted cambric and a Spanish pelisse in dark green shot sarcenet with a small poke bonnet, which framed her russet curls, stepped out of the carriage in some trepidation. Mrs Osborne's footman, having let down the carriage steps for her, trod majestically up to the front door of Mrs Gainford's house and knocked. Amelia, watching from behind the curtains upstairs in the drawing-room was impressed—as Mrs Osborne had meant her to be.

'She's here, dear Augusta,' she breathed. 'Such a fine carriage too, and a footman.'

These details were not lost on Mrs Gainford who put down her hartshorn as Phyllida was announced and rose to greet her.

'Dear Phyllida! Come and kiss me.'

Phyllida blinked and did so. 'I am happy to see you, ma'am.'

'Amelia, I must introduce you to dear Ambrose's widow. This is Miss Heywood,

44

Phyllida, who resides with me. Now, my dear, come and sit down next to me and we can talk. Amelia will organize some tea for us.' She patted the sofa. Amelia dutifully disappeared.

'I am in the poorest health, you must know,' continued Mrs Gainford, her eyes darting about and taking in every detail of Phyllida's expensive garments, 'and of course I was *shattered* by Ambrose's death. I believe that for a time I was almost *maddened* by grief. My friends were most forbearing, they knew that I was not myself, and hardly responsible for what I said or wrote. I was quite unequal to the least exertion.'

Phyllida murmured her sympathy and wondered cynically what other excuses would be forthcoming for her mother-in-law's neglect of every prompting of duty and good feeling towards her widowed daughter-in-law. She did not believe her protestations for one moment: her mother-in-law's letter had been deliberate and calculating. But there was no point in raking up old wounds. All she wanted now, was the barest acknowledgement and after this dreadful Season was over, she would return to Papa and, she hoped, never set eyes on her mother-in-law again.

Mrs Gainford had brightened at Phyllida's sympathy. 'Of course you suffered a blow too,' she added condescendingly, 'and you have been most dutiful in looking after your father, have you not?'

'I love my father,' said Phyllida stiffly.

'Naturally, my dear. You loved your father and wished to stay by his side. Everybody must honour you for that.' She stopped and fiddled with the fringe on her dress for a moment. 'So it cannot be wondered at if we have not met before.'

Phyllida saw Mrs Gainford's mind very clearly. She was ready to acknowledge her, now that Mrs Osborne had taken her up and it would be awkward not to. Wanted to, that is, if no shadow of blame could be attached to her for neglecting to acknowledge her before.

As if to confirm Phyllida's thoughts Mrs Gainford then added, 'With a grandmother of Mrs Osborne's consequence behind you, now, you will have some standing in the world. You will soon be settled I daresay. You must not think that I shall mind. Oh no, a husband and a family will be the very thing for you.'

Phyllida's brows contracted suddenly, as if in pain, but she said nothing.

'Now that your grandmother has magnanimously decided to let bygones be bygones I am sure that it won't be long before I read of another little announcement in the *Morning Post*,' she finished coquettishly.

Mrs Gainford stopped suddenly, for Phyllida was looking at her with so stern an expression on her face and so searching a look in her eyes, now as cold as emerald ice, that she could say no more.

46

At this opportune moment the butler brought in the tea tray, followed by Amelia.

'Ah, dearest Amelia.' Mrs Gainford sank back against the cushions and gave her cousin an imploring glance. 'My hartshorn, if you please.'

Amelia took one look at Phyllida's stormy face and said quickly, 'Certainly Augusta. Mrs Ambrose, some tea? May I offer you a slice of this delicious plum cake?'

Phyllida declined the cake but accepted the tea. Amelia watched her anxiously. Augusta had spoken of her as if she were a mere country bumpkin without intelligence or countenance, but plainly that was not the case. God forbid that she should have suspected anything.

Phyllida leaned forward. 'Tell me, Miss Heywood. I only knew Ambrose for a few months. What was he like before I met him? He told me that he had been very wild.'

'He ... he ...' stuttered Amelia, throwing an agonized look at her cousin. 'He was dashing, certainly.'

'Always very good-looking, even as a little boy,' said Mrs Gainford, dabbing at her eyes.

'And popular with the ladies?'

Amelia's cup rattled in its saucer and in the flurry of mopping up and Amelia's disjointed exclamations at her carelessness, the subject was dropped. But Phyllida's suspicions were aroused. There was something being hidden from her, she was sure. Miss Heywood's unease was almost palpable and far more than upsetting a little tea would seem to warrant.

'I do not know whether I shall see much of you,' said Mrs Gainford, when Phyllida rose to go. 'My poor health, you know. But when we do meet I hope that you will come over and say a few words.'

'Certainly,' said Phyllida coolly, 'I see no reason why we should not be civil.'

Amelia escorted her downstairs. Phyllida eyed her speculatively and then said, 'Miss Heywood, I have the oddest feeling that I have not heard the whole story.'

'The whole story? What whole story?'

'That is what I should like to know.'

Amelia stopped on the stairs and seized Phyllida's hand, clasping it convulsively. 'No, no, my dear Mrs Gainford. You are quite wrong. Believe me, it would be the gravest mistake ... I mean ... you are so intelligent, I can see that ... you would be most unhappy ... everybody would be ... I implore you, do not ask.'

Phyllida disengaged her hand gently and smiled reassuringly into Amelia's frightened eyes. 'I shall not do anything precipitate, you may be sure of that, Miss Heywood. But all the same, I have the right to know.'

* * *

When Hereward and Thorold called the

following morning to collect Araminta and Phyllida, for their ride in the Park, it was not only Phyllida who was a trifle abstracted. Araminta, looking bewitching in a bright blue velvet riding habit with cuffs *à la militaire* and a small riding hat of black beaver, greeted Hereward and Thorold prettily, but her mind was far away.

That morning she had received her first posy—pink roses in a silver filigree holder, and they were from Antony Herriot. The note that accompanied them had been unexceptionable, merely the good wishes of an old friend for a triumphant Season, and even Mrs Osborne had said, 'A very pretty attention, my dear. Just as he ought,' and decided that the £50 for his birthday should be increased to a hundred.

But there had been another note tucked in among the roses, which had read quite differently: *They say there are rope-dancers, jugglers and sword-swallowers at Vauxhall. What do you think, sweetest Araminta? Would you care to come with me to see them? Remember how we played truant and went to the Tower? A.*

Antony had judged well. Nothing could have appealed more to Araminta's unsophisticated taste. A stolen meeting—and all the delights of a fun-fair! The fact that Grandmama had pronounced Vauxhall Pleasure Gardens 'vulgar' put the seal on it. She *would* go. It only remained to meet Antony

49

at the Telfords' party and arrange it.

It crossed her mind fleetingly that this was a very different outing to the one to the Tower that she and Antony had stolen one afternoon about five years ago when she was twelve, her hair in pig-tails and he a spindly youth newly down from Cambridge, but she was easily able to dismiss it. It was all Phyllida's fault: she should be more interested in her doings instead of dismissing her with a 'go away, Araminta, I have to *think*'. Think! Whoever wanted to think when there were all the delights of parties and new clothes and beaux? If Phyllida had been the least bit interested she might have told her. What a pity Belinda wasn't here. It would have made it much more amusing to have a friend to giggle with about this secret excursion.

The four set off down Piccadilly towards Hyde Park, Phyllida dutifully allowing Hereward and Araminta to go in front. She looked about her with a determined enjoyment: to spoil everybody's pleasure by her abstraction would be a very ill-bred thing to do. Besides, however could she explain her unease? It had been a late spring and banks of daffodils and crocuses were still flowering in the Park.

'Oh, how pretty!' she exclaimed, suddenly washed with a wave of homesickness.

'Yes,' said Thorold, and then added gloomily, 'at home now all the bluebells will be out in the Home Wood.'

'I expect you miss them.'

'I do,' he sighed. 'This year Caroline will be able to walk to see them. Last year I had to carry her.'

'Caroline?'

'My daughter. She's nearly one and a half.'

Phyllida swallowed and looked away for a moment before saying, 'An enchanting age. It will be nice for you in a few years' time when you will be able to bring her to Town to see all the sights. Astley's Circus, I expect she'll love that.'

Thorold brightened up. 'Of course. Anyway, as you say, she is too young just now. I miss her but while I'm here I can have some work done on some book bindings. Several of my books have their spines all cracked and the leather has gone in places.'

Phyllida had not lived with a recluse of a father all her life for nothing. She could talk intelligently of vellum and calfskin and the merits of each and discuss which books should be recovered and which repaired. Thorold was concerned about his great-grandfather's much-worn volumes of Ovid's *Metamorphoses, Elegies and Letters* (and presumably the *Ars Amatoria*, though this he did not mention). Should they be re-bound in the same black, or should he choose something else? Red and gold perhaps, what did Mrs Gainford think?

Thorold relaxed in Phyllida's intelligent and unalarming company. He thought gratefully that she made a fellow feel quite at ease. He looked ahead to where Hereward and Araminta were cantering along the grass and his confidence began to ebb away. Araminta, laughing and merry, reminded him of Caroline. How pretty and lively she was! No wonder she did not want to talk to him, she must find him a veritable stick-in-the-mud. He wondered what it was that Hereward had said to make her laugh and he wished suddenly that it could be him. But he could never make anybody laugh, except Drusilla, and even then he had had to tell her it was a joke before she smiled dutifully.

He jerked his thoughts back to Phyllida and a chance reference to butterflies led them to another topic, this time one that Phyllida knew rather better.

'As a boy,' said Thorold, 'I tried to breed silkmoths. Without much success, I'm afraid.'

'We manage it sometimes,' replied Phyllida. 'My father is a keen lepidopterist, you know. I'm particularly fond of the Indian Tree of Heaven Silkmoth—those wonderful dusky colours with touches of pink and mauve.'

'How do you do it, Mrs Gainford? Mine always died.'

'We feed ours on lilac and privet, but they do need to be kept warm. A sudden drop in temperature at the larval stage can be fatal.'

52

Hereward and Araminta had reached a small knoll and reined in. Hereward looked back at Thorold and Phyllida, still talking earnestly, their mounts walking quietly side by side and felt suddenly unaccountably dissatisfied. Araminta was lively and good company, he could not complain of being bored. And yet, how young she was! What she had to say she said with enjoyment and lack of affectation, unlike many débutantes who could be quite brassy in their efforts not to appear naïve. Youth and inexperience were enchanting—but for a short while only, then they became tedious. He looked across at Phyllida and then shook his head quickly as if to rid himself of an unwanted thought. Whatever was the matter with him? He must be growing old. No, what he needed was an evening with Emma.

Araminta too had been looking in Thorold's and Phyllida's direction. 'I wish I could do that,' she said wistfully, her little face looking pensive for once.

'Do what, Miss Stukeley?'

'Talk seriously without being teased all the time. As if I were truly grown-up.'

'Come now,' said Hereward, smiling down at her, 'I daresay my brother and your cousin are discussing the influence of Greek architecture on the plays of Euripides, or some such stuff. Thorold is a very serious person, you know. Sometimes I can hardly understand him myself!'

'Now you are laughing at me again,' protested Araminta, giggling.

Phyllida watched Lord Hereward as he talked to Araminta. She found that she could not help looking at him and such a realization annoyed her, for the resentment at his behaviour the afternoon of the call lingered and she did not like finding him an attractive man. He was very good-looking, she had to admit it. She was uneasily conscious of it and it spelled 'danger'.

A younger Phyllida, naïve and hopelessly in love, had not known, how could she? that the overwhelming physical attraction she had felt on meeting Ambrose had had nothing to do with love and everything to do with her own hungers and needs. An older Phyllida, widowed now and wiser, knew it very well. Ambrose had made love to her with an experience and enthusiasm that had at first frightened and then exhilarated her. She knew his unsteadiness in other directions, but it meant nothing in the hectic whirl of those few months. Love was everything. It was only long afterwards that Phyllida began to realize that passion had blinded her to practically every disadvantage of her situation.

Looking at Hereward now, his fair curls glinting in the sun and his blue eyes smiling down at Araminta, she knew herself to be in danger. Never again would she court the

54

humiliations that had been hers after Ambrose's death, by flinging herself where her heart beckoned—without the informed consent of her head. And her head informed her very clearly that Hereward wouldn't even look twice in her direction: he did not even like her. She was not at all sure that she liked him. Ladies did not have the sort of passions that she knew could sway her all too easily. They did not. The unfortunate fact that he was too attractive for her peace of mind must not be allowed to waft her down some primrose path. Not again.

But somehow the four riders' unspoken thoughts were heeded, though none of them would have admitted them openly, for on the way back, Phyllida found that Araminta had cantered ahead with Thorold and she was left to walk sedately alongside Lord Hereward.

Having once raised the ghost of her late husband, Phyllida could not get him out of her mind. So when, some minutes later, Hereward asked her why she was in such a brown study she replied, more unguardedly than she meant to, 'I was thinking about Ambrose. My mother-in-law invited me to tea yesterday and I realized while I was there that I really knew very little about him.' She laughed a little unsteadily. 'Odd, isn't it, to say about one's husband. But I only knew him for a few months. We met in February, while I was staying with my godmother in Brighton, and by June he was dead. I had the curious feeling that the Ambrose I thought I knew and the Ambrose that Mrs Gainford was talking about could not possibly be the same man.'

Hereward turned in the saddle to look at her. 'You must have met him before, in London, perhaps?'

'No, indeed.'

'I find that difficult to believe. No stolen meetings in Gloucestershire then? Surely people nowadays don't rush into marriage in so precipitate a way?' A girl like you, he wanted to add, who seems on the surface to be so honest and open? Surely you must be different underneath to be wedded with so notorious a gambler and libertine in such immodest haste?

Phyllida smiled gently at the memory of her younger self. 'I'm afraid I was just such a precipitate person. I was naïve ... in love ... and then there was the threat of war. I daresay it seems incredible to you but I assure you that's how it was.'

Hereward shook his head, but did not pursue the subject. 'Your cousin will be an instant success on her come-out,' he said instead.

Phyllida's heart cooled rapidly. Araminta, of course. He was only interested in Araminta. 'Yes, I do hope so. She is so pretty and my grandmother has such hopes of her.'

'Of you too, I daresay.'

'I hope not,' cried Phyllida. 'Grandmama

knows my thoughts on *that* subject.'

There could be no mistaking the passionate sincerity with which she spoke. In spite of himself Hereward's curiosity was aroused. What an extraordinary girl. He had never met anyone at all like her. However did she come to marry Ambrose Gainford and why was she determined not to repeat the matrimonial experiment?

They had now reached Stanhope Gate, close to Apsley House and stopped talking while they negotiated the crossing into Piccadilly. Phyllida's mind went back to the conversation with Mrs Gainford. Something was going on, she was sure of it. Her suspicions seemed confirmed by Lord Hereward's polite incredulity over her marriage. Mrs Gainford had tried to insinuate that, but for the magnanimity of herself and Mrs Osborne, Phyllida would be in disgrace. She was trying to throw the blame for something on to Phyllida's shoulders. But blame for what? To marry in haste might be unwise, but it was hardly a crime. She was perfectly entitled to have a season in London if she pleased. There was nothing in her birth or breeding to preclude it: her father's family was poor, but it was respected.

'... of course, you will be going?'

'I'm sorry, my lord, did you say something? I'm afraid I was not attending.'

Ladies whom he honoured with his attention

normally did not allow their minds to wander. Hereward was not only curious now, he was piqued. Mrs Ambrose Gainford needed a lesson, he thought. He would put his mind to it.

*　　*　　*

Mrs Osborne, as might be expected, demanded Phyllida's instant attendance in her boudoir the moment she was changed out of her riding habit, for she wanted a full account of the morning's ride. Phyllida was guiltily aware that things had not quite gone according to her grandmother's grand design. What was she to say? Indeed, why should she say anything? She was there as Araminta's chaperone, not her gaoler. Phyllida felt a sudden sympathy with her mother who had had to flee Mrs Osborne's importunities in order to marry the man she loved.

She went upstairs towards her room and found Araminta hovering on the landing. 'I hope you enjoyed your ride with Lord Hereward, Phyl,' she began.

'Yes,' said Phyllida cautiously. 'I hope my riding with him did not interrupt anything?'

'Oh, no, no! In fact I was quite pleased to be relieved of his company. He's very agreeable and good-looking, I know that, but somehow I prefer Lord Gifford. He's quiet, but I don't find him dull. He *listens* to me. Lord Hereward only laughs at what I say.' She paused, the skirts of her riding habit looped up over one arm, 'You won't mention this to Grandmama, will you, Phyl? She might decide that Lord Gifford was the better match for me—poor man, I wouldn't want him to be hounded, and he would be!'

Araminta smiled conspiratorially at Phyllida and went into her room, where she promptly forgot Thorold in contemplation of her pink roses and the secret note from Antony.

Phyllida rang the bell for her maid and looked sternly at her reflection in the glass. Quite as much as Araminta she wanted the events of that morning suppressed. It would do no good for Lord Hereward's degree of interest in her to become anything more than that of a courteous man towards a dowdy widow— either in her own mind, or that of her grandmother. He was plainly taken with Araminta, let that be the substance of her report.

Consequently, when she finally tapped on Mrs Osborne's door, her version of the morning (and Araminta's subsequent version over luncheon) bore little resemblance to the facts.

'Lord Hereward was most attentive to Araminta. They rode on ahead and we could hear them laughing and talking.'

Mrs Osborne smiled triumphantly. 'I knew it would be so,' she said. 'If I had decided on

59

Lord Gifford now, I should have had to give him a hint of where my wishes lay. But Lord Hereward, I am sure, is quite capable of doing his courting himself. I do not doubt that we shall see them both here often enough now.'

Phyllida could only be thankful that she had prevaricated.

'And you, my dear,' continued Mrs Osborne belatedly, 'I trust you enjoyed the ride.'

'Yes, thank you, Grandmama.'

'What did you discuss with Lord Gifford?'

'Butterflies,' replied Phyllida blandly, casting down her eyes to hide the gleam of ironic amusement in them. But Mrs Osborne, having no sense of humour, was impervious to irony. She regarded Phyllida and Lord Gifford with a benevolent lack of interest. Lord Gifford was the settled widower; his role was to play the part of an escort for Phyllida while she chaperoned Araminta. It never occurred to her that two minor characters in this particular scene might have stepped out of line.

Her sense of her own rightness was so strong that, as Antony Herriot had discovered, she was fatally easy to deceive.

CHAPTER THREE

Emma Winter sat on her silk-covered *chaise-longue* and surveyed the Adam wallpaper with its Etruscan design and the ornate gilt girandoles with distaste. Sometimes she thought she'd die of boredom, stuck out here in Chelsea, with everything money could buy— except freedom. She had thought things would be very different when she had first met Hereward a year or so ago. Then she had just finished a season at the Regency Theatre and was heartily tired of the burlettas with their suggestive dances and saucy songs. Sick of playing the palpitating heroine, or, more daring, the young hero in skin-hugging tights and flattering doublets. And most of all, sick to death of the smell of old candle grease and sawdust in the theatre and mice and cooking fat in her shabby rooms off the Strand.

She had known that she was not a good enough actress to play at Covent Garden or Drury Lane, the only two licensed playhouses, but somehow she had thought when she came to London that success and fortune would be only just around the corner. Reality was depressingly different. Hereward had been by no means the first man in her life, but normally they were all subservient to the demands of her work—lovers for Sundays or her occasional in-between seasons breaks.

Hereward had come at a fortunate time for her, when she had strained her back (she had been Roxallana, trying to restrain the lustful advances of the cruel Turk) and subsequently been relegated to the chorus—on their meagre

61

pay. Hereward's offer of his protection had seemed like a god-send. But now eighteen months later, she could hardly believe how stifled and bored she felt, especially as he had forbidden her to consort with her theatrical friends.

This morning she had received a letter from her friend Madame Vestris, about the new Coburg Theatre to be opened the following year.

There is to be a new ballet called, I believe, 'Alzora and Nerine', she wrote, *exactly the thing for you, my sweet. Why don't you write to Dick, who's on the management? Look to your laurels, Emma. If Lord H. hasn't proposed marriage yet, is he ever going to? And if it all finishes, what will you do then? Just now people remember you, but they won't forever.*

Emma frowned down at the letter. She had been so sure that Hereward could be persuaded to marry her sometime. Why not? He had no need to await anyone's fortune for he had his own. He always did as he pleased. She was beautiful and she satisfied him, what more could any man ask for? Surely she wasn't allowing that small mistake in her past to upset all her plans? She had had other lovers, true. But so what? So had half the ladies of Society, if rumour was true. She was perfectly prepared

62

to be faithful—more or less—once they were married.

Her reverie was interrupted by an imperative knocking at her front door. Hereward! Hastily she stuffed the letter into a drawer of her escritoire and bit her lips to redden them.

What a beautiful bitch, thought Hereward, as he entered the room and threw his travelling cloak on to a chair. Beautiful and quite probably false. Did it matter? Not really, at least not for the moment. He wanted only one thing from Emma and that she performed superlatively well.

'Let us go upstairs,' said Emma breathlessly as he came towards her tugging at his cravat.

One of Hereward's greatest attractions, decided Emma hazily some time later, was the lover-like impatience he showed. There had been one finicky old lord in the past who had insisted on having everything just-so, folding his trousers, putting his shoes side by side, until she could have screamed with vexation. Hereward was quite liable to tear her clothes off her in his eagerness, but at least he was always lavish with her dress allowance!

'We fit so well together,' Emma murmured. 'I wish it could be for always.'

Hereward propped himself up on one elbow. 'If it were for always, sweetheart, I'd have to be the only one. What about all your Toms and Dicks and Harrys then?'

'W ... what do you mean?' If Polly had

betrayed her, she'd kill her.

'I don't enquire too closely where you go in the afternoons, Emma. So long as you're discreet. I won't have you hanging round the theatres in the evenings without me, but otherwise...' he shrugged. 'Let us be honest, my love. This arrangement suits both of us. Don't try to turn it into something it isn't.'

Emma considered for a moment a passionate declaration of love and then decided against it. Emotional outbursts bored him, she knew that. She would have to tread more carefully. She bit her lip, there must be *some* way of getting what she wanted.

* * *

A few days before Lady Telford's ball for her twin daughters, Margaret and Lucy, Phyllida and Araminta were invited to tea in order to make the Misses Telfords' acquaintance.

'So much more agreeable if one's daughters know some other girls,' Lady Telford had said.

Phyllida had been expecting a small tea party with the opportunity for some private conversation with Margaret and Lucy, but Lady Telford's 'little tea' was a misnomer. She was, in fact, determined to gather round her those people who, she felt, would be most useful to her daughters, and the granddaughters of Mrs Osborne were plainly on the list. Standing at the door waiting to be introduced Phyllida noticed to her amazement that Lord Hereward was there! Whyever had he come? It was well known that such functions as a debutante's tea party bored him to distraction, and indeed, he was standing against the wall, looking with his usual air of disdain at the gathering.

'My dear,' whispered one of the be-turbaned dowagers to their hostess as Phyllida and Araminta entered, 'however did you persuade Hereward to come? Not that he should need persuading with two such lovely daughters—but all the same...'

'Lady Gifford is Lucy's godmother,' replied Lady Telford.

Looking round, Phyllida could see Lady Gifford over by the window, and presumably she had dragged Hereward with her. He addressed a few words to some man standing next to him, but apart from that quite ignored the company, Phyllida noted, particularly, the blushes and sidelong glances of Lady Telford's artless daughters.

Margaret and Lucy were sitting together on the sofa, their arms around each others' waists. Margaret wore blue and Lucy pink, both with a number of fluttery ribbons and with their hair caught up into loose curls at the top of the head *à la Madonna*. They were pretty girls, but Phyllida couldn't help thinking that they had seen too many paintings by Romney of goddesses in flowing draperies affectionately

65

intertwined in some Grecian landscape.

Araminta moved away to greet an acquaintance and Phyllida moved forward towards the sofa to be introduced.

'Are you looking forward to your come-out, Miss Telford?' she asked politely.

'Oh, yes indeed.'

'Indeed, we are,' added Miss Lucy.

'I must confess that I am a little nervous about Araminta's ball,' said Phyllida smiling. 'I am sure that everything will go without a hitch, but somehow I cannot help worrying about catastrophes with my grandmother's china or the band turning up inebriated!'

Miss Telford looked shocked. 'Mrs Osborne would never let that happen I am sure!'

'You may rely on her,' added Lucy earnestly. She looked up and gave a little start, her hand fluttering to her heart. 'Oh! Lord Hereward, how you startled me!'

Phyllida turned round and gave Hereward what she hoped was a cool smile, though she found, to her annoyance, that her heart was beating quite as fast as Miss Lucy's.

Miss Telford cast a languishing look in Hereward's direction and sighed, 'I am such a timid creature, my lord! We have just been saying that we do not know how we shall go on at our ball. Why there are over three hundred guests coming, and I'm sure I do not know half of them! Indeed, we shall look for your support, my lord. It is so uncomfortable when one does not know many gentlemen.' The statement ended on a slight question, for both Margaret and Lucy hoped to have Lord Hereward as a dancing partner. What a triumph *that* would be! (And what a slap in the face for that red-haired little minx, Araminta Stukeley—for the news of Hereward riding with her in the Park had been relayed to them no fewer than three times by concerned friends.)

'I am sure your admirable mother will introduce you both to many fascinating and eligible men,' replied Hereward coldly, raising his eye-glass and surveying first Margaret and then Lucy through it with a marked lack of enthusiasm. 'Come, Mrs Gainford, I am here to escort you to tea.' He gripped Phyllida's elbow and forced her to rise.

Phyllida, flushed and embarrassed, could not rid herself of that hold without drawing all eyes upon them. She curtseyed to the girls and said something proper, trying to ignore poor Lucy's tears of humiliation.

'Stupid creatures!' Hereward propelled Phyllida into a corner where he sat her down and himself next to her and signalled to a passing footman. Though he had released her arm, she was still tinglingly conscious of the grip of those lean fingers.

When tea had been brought, Phyllida said, in an effort to turn her thoughts, 'You were extremely rude, my lord.'

Hereward raised his eyebrows. 'A couple of silly little chits! What do they possibly matter?'

'Perhaps they are a little foolish, but they are both very young and do not deserve to be so snubbed.'

Hereward gave a short, incredulous laugh. 'Egad, I believe you are criticizing me, Mrs Gainford.'

'Certainly I am. You are a guest in their house.'

'I suppose you think I should waste my time talking to those simpering misses!'

'It wouldn't hurt you,' said Phyllida calmly.

Hereward dragged his chair round to face Phyllida. 'Nobody, Mrs Gainford, *nobody* has ever dared to talk to me as you have just done.' His voice was cold but his eyes were hot and angry.

'That, my lord, is obvious,' retorted Phyllida, her own temper rising. 'I expect you have been over-indulged from the nursery.'

Hereward leaned forward, his eyes blazing. 'I never thought I'd live to pity Ambrose Gainford, having such a goody-goody Miss Preachy to wife! God knows there was plenty of material there for you to practise your damned preaching on. As for you, Mrs Gainford, look to your own conduct before you criticize mine! By rights you should be in the Marshalsea!'

'W ... what?' stammered Phyllida, taken aback.

'Your husband, Mrs Gainford, was responsible for the death of a friend of mine. A death which enriched *him* by a small fortune! Your precious Ambrose took poor Johnny to a gambling hell and *fleeced* him! You do understand that phrase, don't you? Fleece! Just like a sheep. Stripped him of everything he possessed. Oh, I grant you that Johnny was foolish! But he was young and newly come into his inheritance and Gainford saw this. To him he was simply a pigeon ripe for plucking. You, Mrs Gainford, are living on his victim's money!'

'W ... what happened to your friend?' whispered Phyllida, her face suddenly drained of all colour.

'Johnny? He hanged himself from the stairwell. I found the body.'

Hereward left her. Phyllida closed her eyes for one agonized moment. It could not be true? Why had she never heard a word of this before? Surely, so great a scandal would have reached Mrs Osborne and she would never have invited her down to London. Would Ambrose have done such a thing ... so callously? And lived on the proceeds? Surely it could not be so? Nobody knew better than Phyllida that there had been no money to speak of; she had even had to sell Ambrose's fob watch to settle her bill for lodgings in Brussels after his death and buy herself a place on the boat home.

Lord Hereward must be lying! Yes, perhaps

69

because for once somebody had dared to call his manners into question. Could Ambrose really have done that? Phyllida sank back in her chair, thankful that a display of potted palms at least partially concealed her growing distress.

*　　*　　*

Araminta, whose spirits were mercurial, had decided that this was the most boring tea party *ever*. Antony Herriot had not been invited and as she was all keyed up to meet him and arrange a stolen evening, the let-down was severe. She had not yet learned to take disappointments philosophically and, had she not been in company, would have felt very much inclined to throw herself down on the floor and kick and scream, exactly as she had done for many years in the nursery. Now, she no longer had temper tantrums but was quite adept at making everybody around her feel uncomfortable if things did not go her own way. She tossed her copper curls at one of Margaret's remarks, turned a cold shoulder on Lucy, and scowled at Lord Bromsgrove who was rashly attempting a little fatherly dalliance.

'Well, well, who's this fairy then? By Jove, you must be Tom Stukeley's daughter. You have a great look of him, my dear.'

Araminta gave an impatient shrug, which

caused Margaret and Lucy to exchange a speaking look. 'I hardly remember him, except that he had a bristly moustache.'

'In that way there can hardly be any resemblance!' replied Lord Bromsgrove jocularly.

'I didn't like him much,' she added.

'Bless my soul!' Lord Bromsgrove's mild blue eyes blinked.

'He was always telling me to run along.'

Well, thought Lord Bromsgrove, as he moved off in search of more appreciative company, what a little vixen. Badly brought up and pert. Not but that Tom wasn't always an impatient man with his 'go away, there's a good fellow'. Still, she was bound to make a good match, manners or no. Rumour had it that she was worth every penny of £60,000. What a pity his son Ned was still at Eton, otherwise he could have had a touch at this little spitfire.

Araminta helped herself to a meringue, and then to several others, after which her spirits rose. It was at this point that Thorold found her.

'You weren't here before,' said Araminta accusingly, offering him a meringue.

'No, I came late.' Thorold took one gingerly. 'Why?'

'I was in a fight,' said Thorold apologetically.

'A fight!' Now Araminta looked at him she

could see the beginnings of a bruise on his jaw and that one hand had some court plaster over the knuckles. She regarded him with a new interest. 'I didn't even think you could fight!'

'I wasn't very successful,' replied Thorold ruefully.

'Well, what happened?'

'I was coming out of an antiquarian bookshop in the City with Mr Nathan, an old friend of mine. Mr Nathan preceded me, and I think they must have been waiting for him, for he's old and frail. Anyway, two youths jumped on him and I went to his rescue. That's all.'

'Did you call a constable?'

Thorold shook his head, wincing slightly as he did so. 'No point. I felled one of them with a book and had a bit of a turn-up with the other. He escaped eventually, but by the time I'd come to, the first one had escaped as well. You see before you, Miss Stukeley, a pretty poor knight errant!' And then, mindful of his instructions, 'I'm sure my brother would have done far better.'

'Lord errant, surely?'

Thorold laughed suddenly, a deep, rich chuckle, and Araminta joined in.

'And your poor friend?'

'A few bruises. Shocked, poor fellow, but all right, I'm happy to say. I took him home and that is why I am late.'

'I think you were very noble,' said Araminta, her eyes shining.

'*Noblesse oblige*,' said Thorold and chuckled again: he had quite forgotten, contemplating Araminta's admiring green eyes, that he was unable to laugh with pretty young girls.

*   *   *

Emma Winter put two fingers in her mouth and gave a most unladylike whistle. Instantly several casement windows shot up and heads poked out shouting curses in a variety of picturesque ways. It was not long after noon in a little alley just off Henrietta Street near Covent Garden, where one of Emma's friends lived. It was also notorious for its bordellos, which accounted for its generally shuttered air, with only a few yawning chambermaids coming out with their quart jugs to the milk cart.

Emma whistled again and at last the window above her opened, and a face, charmingly framed in a frilled night cap, looked down.

'Oh! Lor' Em, I might have known.' Then indoors, 'Molly! Open the door, it's Miss Winter.'

'What, still abed, Nell?' Emma entered the room and glanced at the bed, which bore the inevitable signs of having been slept in by two people and recently vacated (rather swiftly) by one of them. 'Where's your friend then?'

'Out in the yard under the pump,' said Nell, indicating a chair covered with a gaudy shawl.

'You'll meet him later.' Then she added in a lowered voice, 'Good fun, but no money.'

'God, Nell!' Emma looked round at the cracked plaster and cheap washstand with its chipped jug and bowl, imperfectly disguised by an expensive bouquet thrust into the jug, presumably from an admirer, for Nell never lacked those. 'Why do you live here? Surely you are up enough in the world to find somewhere better?'

Nell shrugged. 'I like it here.'

'It's full of pimps and whores,' retorted Emma, with a fine disregard for her own equivocal position.

'So? They keep theatre hours, though. And you know how late we get after a show, Em. You'd think it would be unsafe here, but it ain't. One of the bully boys next door, Tim Docherty, knows me and sees I don't have any trouble. Mad about the theatre, he is! Says he saw me as Rosara fourteen times!'

Footsteps were heard coming up the stairs, a firm masculine tread and then a muffled squeak and giggle from Molly. Nell raised her eyes briefly to the ceiling. A young man entered, clad only in nether breeches and with a coarse towel around his shoulders. His hair had been roughly dried. Very good-looking, thought Emma approvingly; she liked those warm brown eyes and that lazy smile. His teeth were good too, so often a promising countenance was spoilt by rotten teeth. He

74

smiled at Emma, his eyes travelling over her appreciatively, and looked questioningly at Nell.

'Mr Herriot, Emma. Tony, this is Miss Winter.'

'Ah! The lovely Emma Winter, late of the Regency Theatre?'

'The same.'

'I have heard of you,' said Antony thoughtfully, sitting down on the bed and reaching for his shirt.

'In what connection, may I ask?'

'A *noble* one,' replied Antony.

Emma hid her annoyance that she was known to him only through her position as Hereward's mistress and not in her capacity as 'the brightest jewel of the Regency Theatre' as one admirer had called her. 'Unfortunately, I sustained a back injury while at the theatre,' she said coolly. 'And time out of work does not pay the rent.'

'How can you, Em,' cried Nell. 'Why you were mad for him!' Nell would have given her eye teeth for Lord Hereward and resented Emma's dismissal of him as merely a sound financial investment. She hoped Emma wasn't playing fast-and-loose with him—and from the way she was eyeing Tony it was on the cards—that was surely the way to lose such an out-and-outer.

So this was Lord Hereward's mistress, thought Antony. He'd heard plenty about her from gossip in the club, even seen her from afar, but nothing had prepared him for the smooth silkiness of those black tresses or her flawless creamy skin. What a peach! What was she doing here? Did Lord Hereward know? It hardly seemed likely that he would allow his mistress to visit an alley full of bordellos, even to see a friend. This could be useful. It did not seem possible, but could she be bored, restless or dissatisfied in some way? Else why visit so insalubrious an area? In Antony's view friends were discarded when they had served their turn. From Eton onwards he had traded on his good looks to get what he wanted and then discarded the donor. No doubt Emma was the same. Nell was a sweet creature, but hardly of Emma's current status. Antony's busy mind weaved in and out of various possibilities.

'I met Lord Hereward the other day, Miss Winter,' he said at last, having selected the option he thought might serve his turn.

'Oh? And where was that?'

'At my godmother's house. Mrs Osborne.'

Emma looked up quickly. Ah! thought Antony.

'Yes, Mrs Osborne wanted him to meet her granddaughters, Miss Stukeley and Mrs Gainford.'

'G ... Gainford?'

'Do you know her?'

'No! No.'

'Tiresome woman,' went on Antony with a

76

smile under watchful eyes. 'Always butting in where she isn't wanted. I'm sure you know the sort of creature I mean.'

'Very tedious,' agreed Emma.

'Now I find Miss Stukeley much more amusing, but I am quite cut out, Miss Winter! Mrs Gainford is determined to act the chaperone. Of course, I'm sure she's more complaisant when Lord Hereward is there to show an interest in Araminta. I believe Mrs Osborne has hopes in that direction.'

'How intriguing!' said Emma lightly. She opened her reticule and took out a small notepad and pencil. 'Nell, my love, tell me when your new show opens and then I must be off.'

Nell told her. Emma offered her one scented cheek and Antony a hand, and left.

Antony lay back on the bed and smiled up at the smoke-grimed ceiling. Now that was very clever of him, he thought. Emma Winter was the sort of woman who would be very uneasy at the thought of anybody coming between herself and Lord Hereward. Her position depended on it. He had not committed himself with regard to Araminta, merely dropped a hint that he would remove any threat from Araminta, if she would see to Mrs Gainford. Neither he nor Lady Selina had been able to come up with anything substantial with regard to Phyllida, only Ambrose Gainford's unsavoury reputation, and there was nothing new in that. Nothing he could use to discomfit her. But he felt pretty certain that, having hinted at Lord Hereward's possible interest in Araminta, Emma would come up with something.

*　　*　　*

Phyllida paced up and down in her bedroom that evening after the Telford tea party in an agony of indecision. Was this the scandal that Miss Heywood had implored her not to look into? It seemed likely. And yet, if what Lord Hereward had said was true, why was the whole Gainford family not disgraced? Mrs Gainford was accustomed to come up to Town. She might be thought foolish, but nobody failed to acknowledge her. She, Phyllida, was still acceptable to her grandmother. For Phyllida could not see Mrs Osborne allowing even a breath of scandal to harm Araminta's prospects.

Worst of all, had Ambrose really drawn in an inexperienced young man and deliberately bled him dry? Phyllida stopped her pacing and sank down on the window seat, pressing her hot forehead against the cool glass. What did she really know of Ambrose after all? That he was handsome and charming certainly, and with an inexhaustible flow of high spirits. His faults towards her, if any, were an airy disregard for what he called 'household trivialities'. He would rush her out for a ride on the Downs, never mind that she had arranged for the chimney sweep to call: or later in Belgium, to have an impromptu picnic in the wood at Hougoumont (ironically near the very spot where they had eventually found his body after the battle). Could so impulsive a man have set out to ruin somebody?

As for the accusations about the money, Ambrose never seemed to have any. But then neither did many of his fellow officers. Pay was always in arrears; they were all waiting for a stroke of luck, a win at the races, a parental draft on the bank, and somehow they had lurched from one financial crisis to the next. Phyllida had loved it. After the stresses and strains of her mother's sickbed and having the responsibilities of seeing to the strictest economy thrust upon her at too early an age, it had felt like a blessed release, a catching up on the carefree childhood she had never had. And somehow there always was enough. Somebody filled the pot. A friend brought in some pigeons and a hare, a fellow officer lent Ambrose his spare horse, Mrs Cade bought Phyllida a new cloak and bonnet in the smart Brussels shops.

Phyllida was vaguely aware that they were all whirling in a merry-go-round of uncertainty and frantic activity those last few months and that people's personalities, her own included, were distorted in the pressure. It was only in the long, quiet months afterwards that she was able to acknowledge that, had he lived, Ambrose might have been unreliable as a husband and a provider. But she could not believe him a hard or cruel man.

She had a sleepless night, full of vague and menacing dreams and in the morning decided to tell some part at least of her worries to her grandmother.

'Johnny?' Mrs Osborne raised her thin eyebrows. 'You must mean Johnny Taunton, I suppose.'

'I do not know. I only heard the first name. But when I heard my husband's name mentioned, you may imagine my shock.'

'Who was talking, may I ask?'

'I do not know, Grandmama,' said Phyllida mendaciously. 'They were around the corner, talking low, and I did not wish to be observed. I beg you, please tell me what happened.'

'Nothing you need concern yourself about, my dear Phyllida. Young men will always gamble far more than is good for them.'

'But to kill himself!'

'Phyllida,' said Mrs Osborne sternly, 'it is not *your* affair if a foolish young man killed himself after gambling with a man you weren't yet married to!'

'Of course, Grandmama. I am sorry I disturbed you.' But Phyllida was not satisfied. In one way Mrs Osborne was right—she was not responsible—and yet she did not think that it was as straightforward as her grandmother

80

was suggesting. Lord Hereward's anger had been for something far more serious than mere unlucky gaming.

She considered appealing to Miss Heywood but then discarded it. She really could not discuss the matter with a stranger, even if a cousin by marriage, especially one close to so unsympathetic a woman as her mother-in-law. No, Phyllida straightened her shoulders, she had no choice, it would have to be Lord Hereward himself!

The evening of the Telfords' ball, Phyllida dressed with the greatest care. If she was ever going to tackle Lord Hereward, she would need the confidence of looking her best. She decided to wear her new primrose silk evening dress with its daffodil-yellow satin underskirt. Yellow was a colour that was newly fashionable and very difficult to wear as Miss Lannes had informed Mrs Osborne. But it was a colour that suited Phyllida admirably, turning the red in her hair into a deep chestnut and showing off her fair skin and deep green eyes. Her dress was draped in the Grecian style, which set off her slim figure and gave her a quiet and distinguished elegance.

Phyllida had no jewellery apart from a locket that had belonged to her mother, and this she wore with a gold chain borrowed from Araminta's overstocked jewellery box. She pushed her feet into her yellow kid slippers with silk rosettes and allowed her maid to drape a light shawl over her shoulders.

'Oo, you do look a picture, madam,' said her maid enthusiastically.

'Fine feathers make fine birds,' retorted Phyllida, staring critically at her reflection. Would she do? Would Lord Hereward allow her the opportunity to talk to him? Or would she be a wallflower all evening at this, her first ball, while younger and prettier girls twirled round the floor in their partners' arms? She quickly pushed away the thought that she was as much concerned about Lord Hereward asking her to dance as about him letting her talk.

Araminta, meanwhile, was driving her maid distracted with her indecision. It wasn't until Hetty was nearly in tears, with three dresses discarded on the floor, that Mrs Osborne, dignified in purple velvet and an impressive turban headdress, swept into the room and came to her rescue.

'The pale green, Hetty,' she said commandingly.

'But I wanted to wear my pink!' wailed Araminta, who had in fact discarded it twice already.

'With that hair, child!'

'Well, I like it, so there,' muttered Araminta.

'Nonsense, Araminta. You will oblige me by wearing the green. Both charming and unusual and it will set off your hair. Really, I am most unlucky in both my granddaughters having hair of so vulgar a red.' Her voice gave the impression that if she had been vouchsafed a word with the Almighty, such a sartorial solecism would have been avoided. 'However, you cannot help it and we must make the best of it.'

Still muttering, Araminta allowed Hetty to slip her dress on over her head, and under Mrs Osborne's stern eye stopped fidgeting while the maid did up the tiny silk buttons.

'That is better.' Mrs Osborne turned to go. 'And your pearls, Araminta, don't forget your pearls.'

The Telfords' house in Grosvenor Square was resplendent with lights as Mrs Osborne's carriage drew up outside the portico. A red carpet had been rolled out from the front door to protect the guests' footwear from the dirt of the street, and lanterns were hung along the railings. Two footmen were there to let down the carriage steps and assist the ladies to alight.

The ballroom, built at the back of the house by the previous Lord Telford, was decorated with great bowls of flowers, and the candles in the cut-glass chandeliers reflected thousands of prisms, sending rainbow sparkles over the ceiling. There was a small orchestra on the dais at one end and chairs around the edge for dowagers and chaperones, or any young lady unfortunate enough to be without a partner.

A footman bowed and handed Phyllida and Araminta a dance card each, and tiny gold pencils with tassels attached. Phyllida looked at Mrs Osborne.

'Ought I...' she began, aware of two contradictory thoughts. One was that she was a chaperone and must spend the evening on one of those hard-looking chairs, and the other that Lord Hereward must ask her to dance.

'Nonsense, Phyllida,' said Mrs Osborne exasperated. 'Of course you must dance. Araminta needs no chaperone but myself tonight.'

Phyllida took the dance card but thought perhaps no one will want to dance with me anyway.

In this she was wrong. A new and elegantly beautiful girl must always be noticed: one who was Mrs Osborne's granddaughter was not going to be cold-shouldered. Phyllida did not know it, but Mrs Osborne had paved the way by dropping a few words in the ear of her friend, Lady Albinia Marchmont, whose discreetly indiscreet tongue she could rely on— 'Dear Cecilia Osborne will dower Phyllida Gainford, I understand ... ten thousand, I believe...'

Only Lady Selina Lemmon had had the malice to retort, 'About a quarter of what Phyllida Gainford could have expected if her mother had not made that foolish marriage to Herbert Danby!'

Antony Herriot stood against a pillar and waited until the first throng of admirers surrounding Araminta had been promised their dances. He caught her glancing at him once or twice but made no move towards her. He judged that coolness would best further his suit, not eagerness. Ah, so Mrs Gainford was dancing too this evening. Capital! That gave him more opportunity to whisk Araminta away somewhere private for a while without any interference. He turned to examine the long French windows behind him. Good, the heavy draped curtains would certainly mask any exits. One had a key in the door. Antony tried the handle gently. It was locked. Quietly he extracted the key and slid it into his pocket.

When Lord Hereward and the Earl of Gifford arrived with their grandmother, nobody could have watched their progress more carefully than Mrs Osborne. Ah, the Earl was looking their way—hopefully, she thought, and Phyllida was very properly studying the sticks of her fan. Lord Hereward, tiresome man, was looking with his usual air of cool disdain at a marble nymph in an alcove, draped in gauze for the ball, presumably in an excess of modesty by Lady Telford, an effect, thought Mrs Osborne, which was far more eye-catching and infinitely more salacious than if she had been left in her original nudity. But it was all right. Having very properly greeted their hostess and presumably written their names on Margaret and Lucy's dance cards, Thorold, Hereward and their grandmother made their way slowly towards her.

Phyllida and Araminta rose as Lady Gifford approached them, Araminta offering her ladyship her chair. Thorold warmly requested a couple of dances from Phyllida and then, more diffidently, from Araminta. Now Hereward, after a cool bow to Phyllida, was asking Araminta. Phyllida could not bear it and looked away.

At that moment Lady Albinia sailed up with a portly young gentleman in tow, whom she introduced as her nephew, Barnabas Marchmont. Barnabas, a very correct young man, bowed stiffly to Phyllida and Araminta and, as low as his corset would allow, to Mrs Osborne. Phyllida, in an agony of impatience, could see Hereward still talking to Araminta. Any minute he would go, and he must not! She must talk to him about Johnny Taunton, she must!

Now Barnabas was bowing again in front of Phyllida and requested a dance. 'One of the country dances, Mrs Gainford, or perhaps we might attempt the Boulanger. I fear I am somewhat old-fashioned and do not waltz.'

Phyllida could only be thankful. Being clasped to that protuberant stomach was not something she could view with equanimity. She took up her pencil and wrote down his initials.

When she looked up, Hereward had gone.

Antony Herriot, watching from across the

room, saw that both Phyllida and Araminta were now being led on to the floor and that a seat beside Mrs Osborne was empty. So much the better, he thought; a little time spent in flattering the old lady would prevent a rearguard action. He began to move towards them.

Lady Gifford leaned forward towards Mrs Osborne. 'How attractive both your granddaughters look tonight,' she said.

'Thank you. Araminta is very pretty in spite of that hair.'

'Mrs Gainford too. Really, I would hardly recognize her as the lady in the old-fashioned black crêpe I met at your house only a few weeks ago.' She sighed. 'Let us hope she finds happiness again. Poor Ambrose Gainford was sadly unsteady.'

'I have her under my eye this time,' replied Mrs Osborne. 'But at the moment she declares that she will not re-marry! She must be brought to see that that is mere foolishness.' She looked across the ballroom to where Phyllida was dancing with Thorold. Thorold was talking in an animated way and Phyllida listening with every appearance of interest.

Lady Gifford followed Mrs Osborne's gaze for one thoughtful moment and then said, 'Caution, Cecilia. The birds are very shy.'

No more needed to be said. Both ladies understood each other very well. Mrs Osborne, however, was encouraged and was able to greet

Antony with a hopeful mind and to enjoy his gossip and little flatteries. Like most elderly ladies she liked personable young men, and she was quite convinced that Antony knew his place. Accordingly, when Araminta and her partner returned, she was able to accept his teasing of her granddaughter and raised no objection to him asking her to dance.

The evening wore on. Phyllida danced every dance. If her having been married to a good-for-nothing was looked on askance by the older generation, the fact that Mrs Osborne sponsored her was enough to allay their qualms. Her manners were unaffected, Lady Gifford was seen talking to her, and she was allowed to be a 'charming, sweet girl'.

Phyllida did not hear these accolades, whispered from one dowager to another, behind curled ostrich fans, but she had the gratifying knowledge that her dance card was full. Even if Lord Hereward did not wish to dance with her, she would not have the mortification of being a wallflower in his eyes.

She was just wondering (removing herself from Mr Marchmont's too close clasp) whether she might write to Hereward and then deciding that such conduct would be too scandalous, when fate took a hand in the affair.

Mr Marchmont, on whom his host's excellent champagne had had an exhilarating effect, attempted the *pas de Zéphyr* with rather too much energy and descended heavily on

Phyllida's hem. There was a tearing sound and Phyllida looked down to see a stretch of her lace frill hanging free.

Mr Marchmont was profuse in his apologies. Phyllida smilingly replied that it was nothing, she could repair it in a trice. She retreated to the ladies' retiring room and began to search for the little packet of pins in her reticule. Mr Marchmont mopped his brow and retreated thankfully towards the refreshments, conscious suddenly of a tight corset and restricting neck-tie.

Phyllida emerged some time later into the cool and quiet of the hall and stood there for a moment or two in the shade of a large fern, grateful for the fresh air, for the candles of the ballroom, though of the finest wax, were becoming smoky and hot and made her eyes sting. It was then that she noticed Hereward, leaning against the plinth of a marble statue of yet another nymph, holding a glass of wine in his hand. He was watching her, but said nothing.

Without giving herself time to think, she said, 'Lord Hereward, may I have a word with you?'

He looked at her with icy blue eyes and said in a cool voice, 'Certainly Mrs Gainford.'

'N ... not now,' said Phyllida hurriedly, losing her calm under that cold stare. 'I ... I mean, whenever is convenient to you.'

'Now is perfectly convenient.'

Phyllida looked around but the hall was deserted. He was obviously not going to give her a more private moment. While her courage was high she went on, 'I have been thinking about what you were saying the other day. I wanted to ask you more about that dreadful business. I tried to talk to my grandmother about it, but she was not very helpful.' Phyllida did not want to say that Mrs Osborne had found it of small importance and dismissed it. 'I should like to know the truth of what happened, and I believe that you could give it to me.'

Hereward put his half-empty glass down in the plinth and looked at Phyllida. Was there carefully concealed surprise in that look? 'I see,' he said, after a pause. 'Are you thinking of returning the money to his wretched family, Mrs Gainford?'

'There was no money, my lord. At least not that I am aware of. I do not believe that I ever had more than a few guineas from my husband. I am very sure that he had none. All the officers in his regiment were in the same case. We all lived from day to day. When he was killed I had to sell his watch to pay off our landlady and get a passage on the boat.'

Hereward felt acutely uncomfortable. She could not be speaking the truth and yet he could not disbelieve her. Those large, green eyes were without guile.

'Where was your husband in 1814?'

'I do not know.' Phyllida looked startled. 'I know that he was in the Peninsula and was invalided home, but I think that that was earlier.'

'It was. The wounded hero. He used that line, among many others, with Johnny.'

'And ... and after?'

'There was a scandal, of course. Your husband disappeared. Perhaps to Gloucestershire, Mrs Gainford?'

Phyllida took a step back and said in a low, passionate voice, 'Why will you never believe me? Why must I be responsible for the death of a man I never knew and the gambling of a man I was not yet married to? Why are you so unfair, so unjust? What have *you* got to hide, Lord Hereward?'

Hereward started, but before he could say anything, Phyllida, her head high, swept past him back into the ballroom. Hereward grasped his half-empty wine glass, drained it, and then realized that he had just snapped the stem of it in two.

* * *

Antony led Araminta on to the dance floor and whispered as they prepared to take their places, 'Shall we contrive a little accident with your train so that we may make some private arrangements? Or have you decided, my sweet, to be a good girl this Season?'

Araminta's eyes sparkled with mischief, the pleasure enhanced by possible discovery. Quite as much as the forbidden outings, Araminta enjoyed the intrigue that preceded them. Often the excursion itself fell sadly flat after the excitement of planning it. 'I've always wanted to see Vauxhall,' she declared. 'Grandmama says that it is too rowdy nowadays, but I think she is just being stuffy.'

'It can become a little free.' Antony remembered with a reminiscent sigh various strolls in the Dark Walk with Nell, soon after they had first met. The arbours and sylvan grottoes were perfect places for innocent and not-so-innocent pleasurable activities.

'Pooh!' retorted Araminta. 'I cannot see how anybody can harm me if you are there.'

Antony smiled but said nothing.

In the event, Araminta did not need to arrange anything; an unwary jog from a passer-by and a glass of champagne splashed on to her skirt. Swiftly, Antony took her arm and solicitously removed her to the French windows. He guided her behind the curtains, took the key out of his pocket, motioned her outside and locked the door behind them.

Araminta was impressed. The callow youths who had taken her and Belinda to the circus from their Bath seminary had been far less cool, indeed one of them had been positively shaking with nerves. The schoolgirl admiration she had always had for Antony now flared up into a rosy glow. How handsome he was!

The balcony was a wide one and a stone flight of steps curved from it down into the garden, now quiet and silver in the moonlight. Antony led her to a wrought-iron bench out of sight of the house and they sat down. Eagerly, Araminta told him that Mrs Osborne invariably played quadrille with some friends on Wednesday evenings, allowing Phyllida to chaperone her if necessary. However, in two weeks' time Phyllida had been invited to the opera by Lady Gifford. Araminta, seeing she might decline, had done so thankfully. It was on a Wednesday, so that she would be quite alone. She was sure she could evade any commitments for that evening; a simple cold, a headache, there could be no problem.

'How will you leave the house without being seen?' enquired Antony, realizing with some exasperation that so far Araminta had made all the arrangements.

'I shall wear my old cloak and slip out of the side door. It squeaks but I shall oil it.'

'And getting back?'

'I shall take the key, silly.'

'Very well, we shall make final arrangements nearer the time. If you need to contact me, a note to White's will find me.'

They talked for some minutes more, Antony pondering whether the moment was ripe for some amorous overture. He didn't want to

93

frighten her. Araminta, in all the ardours of a first falling in love wondered if Antony was just being kind as to a little sister, or whether he too felt this wonderful intoxication.

'Antony?' she began tentatively, putting one gloved hand on his sleeve.

Antony, turning, read the message in those pleading green eyes and trembling lips and bent his head to kiss her.

CHAPTER FOUR

The morning after the ball Lord Hereward visited his club. White's, the most fashionable men's club, was patronized by men of distinction as well as fashion, and Hereward hoped to find Sir Marmaduke Vavasour there.

'Sir Marmaduke in?' he enquired of the flunkey who opened the door and relieved him of his hat, gloves and cane.

'Yes, my lord. In his usual chair with the *Morning Post*, I believe, my lord.'

General Sir Marmaduke Vavasour was now in his sixties. White-haired and inclined to gout, he was still a force to be reckoned with at the War Office. As a staunch Tory he had supported Wellington's policy of continuing the war against Napoleon. Events had justified him, and as he had a shrewd grasp of the internal politics of the War Office, he was now something of an *éminence grise*, and his opinions sought after.

His grandmother moving in strict Tory circles, Hereward had, of course, known Sir Marmaduke from the cradle.

'Ha! my boy. Glad to see you.' Sir Marmaduke looked up from his paper. 'Thank you, I'll join you for coffee. Damned doctor tells me to cut down on the alcohol. Gout, you know. Plaguey nuisance.'

Hereward signalled to a waiter and then fetched a cushion for Sir Marmaduke's foot, which was resting, swathed in bandages, on a small footstool.

'I was wanting to ask your opinion, sir,' said Hereward, when they were settled. 'Do you recall a Captain Gainford? Captain Ambrose Gainford.'

'What of him?' growled Sir Marmaduke. 'Thought he was dead.'

'Yes, at Waterloo. I want to know what he was doing in 1814.'

'With his regiment, I presume.'

Hereward shook his head. 'I think not. He was wounded in '13. Quite seriously, I think. He was involved in a scandal late that year with an old friend of mine, Johnny Taunton, you may recall.'

'Ah yes.' Sir Marmaduke shot him a look from under bushy white eyebrows. 'Bad business that.'

'Gainford won a lot of money—over ten

thousand. The next I know of him he was back with his regiment early in '15.'

'So what do you want to know? Do you think he cheated, is that it?'

'I don't think so, though he may have. Poor Johnny had not the least flair for cards.'

Sir Marmaduke finished the rest of his coffee and then said seriously, 'Leave it, Hereward.'

'I'm sorry, sir. But I shall be discreet in my enquiries.'

There was a pause. Sir Marmaduke stared reflectively into his coffee cup. 'Very well, then. But this is for your ears only. I don't suppose it matters now, for the poor chap is dead. We had evidence that Taunton was selling information.'

'Johnny, a spy! It cannot be true!' It was Gainford who was the villain: it could never be Johnny!

'I'm afraid it was.' Sir Marmaduke shook his head sadly. 'I gather Taunton ran up gaming debts at Oxford and needed money. His father always kept him very short, you know. A clutch-fist! You send a boy up to Oxford to see a bit of life, meet the right people! It's not a time to keep him short of the ready. Always blamed the father as much as the son myself. But, there it is. Of course, Taunton was in no position to tell the French much: fortunately for us, Napoleon's spies were, in the main, incompetent. But he could have become an embarrassment, especially when his father died and he came on the Town.'

'So from the War Office's point of view his death was provident?'

'Quite.'

'Perhaps even ... expected?'

Sir Marmaduke looked at him sternly. 'This country is a parliamentary democracy, not an imperial dictatorship!'

True, thought Hereward, but you still have not answered my question.

* * *

Nell stood by the entrance to the jewellers in South Audley Street and watched the tall and unmistakable figure of Lord Hereward FitzIvor come out of the shop. He strode off in the direction of Bond Street. Lucky Emma, thought Nell wistfully. She could fancy such a man, and he wasn't stingy with his presents either. She turned and went into the jewellers.

M. Tessier came forward as soon as she entered and, after a few low-murmured words, ushered her into a private room behind a grey-felt curtain. Nell had a well-established relationship with M. Tessier. She was extravagant, money never stayed in her pocket, and her admirers were always buying her jewellery. M. Tessier gave her a fair price for her bits and pieces and in return Nell mentioned the Tessier name to her would-be lovers.

'That was Lord Hereward, was it not?' she asked, when business was concluded.

'Ah yes, he has just bought one of my most exquisite little posy holders. He must have a young lady in his eye, do you not think so, mademoiselle?'

An expensive trifle, thought Nell. The recipient was hardly likely to be Emma: he had no need to court her with flowers. She slipped her guineas into her beaded purse, thanked M. Tessier and left the shop. After a few moments' reflection she set off in the direction of Bond Street. There was only one florist there she knew of. It would be interesting to see to whom Lord Hereward was sending this pretty (and expensive) gift.

Nell was a good-natured girl and fond of Emma, but she owned to some resentment, especially when Tony had spent quite twenty minutes asking about her after she had gone. And he had not been to visit her since! Emma did not deserve Lord Hereward, and that was a fact!

When Nell reached the florist's shop it was empty save for a tired-looking assistant sweeping the floor. Nell rapped smartly on the desk. The assistant straightened up wearily, and after untying his apron very slowly, came over.

'I want to know,' she said, putting a shilling down on the table in front of her and tapping it with one pretty finger, 'which lady Lord

Hereward FitzIvor has been sending flowers to.'

'Eh?'

Nell began to repeat the question, but then caught sight of a leather-bound order book. She leant over the desk, turned it round to face her and opened it.

''Ere,' cried the assistant, 'you can't do that!'

Nell picked up the coin and waggled it in front of him. 'Oh, yes I can!' She turned over the pages and then stopped. 'Good heavens! How intriguing!'

'Excuse me, madam,' said the assistant, in a stronger voice this time. 'May I ask what you are doing?'

'Just looking,' said Nell cheekily. She flicked the coin at him and left the shop.

She was fond of Em, she thought, but she'd have to learn that you couldn't play fast and loose with an out-and-outer like Lord Hereward. It would be a positive pleasure to relay such an interesting tit-bit to one of her oldest friends.

*   *   *

Phyllida and Araminta, neither of them caring much for breakfast in bed, even after they had danced into the small hours, came down to the breakfast parlour at the back of the house at about eleven o'clock on the morning after the Telfords' dance. Here Phyllida had some

99

coffee and a slice of toast and Araminta consumed her eggs, bacon, tomatoes and kidneys, followed by muffins and honey and several cups of coffee. Phyllida watched her in awe as she buttered her third muffin and covered it liberally with honey.

'I'm hungry,' said Araminta unnecessarily.

'So I see!'

A number of bouquets had arrived for Araminta. She giggled as she read the accompanying cards and handed them to Phyllida.

'Look, Phyl, Lieutenant Carter wrote me a poem!

Oh Queen of the Ball,
You outshone them all.

How sweet! Who's yours from?'

A large bunch of irises lay beside Phyllida's plate. She handed the card to her cousin.

'Good heavens!' exclaimed Araminta. 'Mr Marchmont! How oddly he writes. Listen to this, Phyl. *A small token, dear Mrs Gainford, of my unutterable esteem for a lady whose beauty is equalled only by the attainments of her mind. In most ladies, attainments of intellect are less pleasing than her domestic capabilities, but I am confident that your superior mental capacities, dear madam, do not preclude the more womanly accomplishments proper to your sex.* What on earth does that mean, do you think?'

'I have the most unnerving feeling that he has decided that I am worthy to be Mrs Barnabas Marchmont—so far as a mere female can presume to judge, of course.'

Araminta giggled. 'But what an odd thing to write after a ball.'

'Perhaps he thinks that his approval must secure my affections?'

'He's a condescending prig!' retorted Araminta.

Phyllida did not pursue the subject. She was feeling rather low and the self-satisfied importance of Mr Marchmont's note had annoyed rather than amused her. Lord Hereward thought ill of her, however unjustly, and the whole evening had been clouded by it. In vain did she remind herself that she had danced every dance and Lady Jersey had been most agreeable when she had been introduced to her, but everything had been overshadowed by that disastrous conversation. Why, oh why, did she ever imagine she might talk to him? How could she ever dare face him again?

She was so absorbed in her reflections that she did not pay much attention to what Araminta was saying.

'... very good-looking, don't you think, Phyl?'

'Oh, yes, certainly,' she replied automatically.

'Even Grandmama likes him, you know, she told me so last night. She said he was "much improved".'

'Grandmama is difficult to please. So if she likes your admirer you may be easy.' Whoever were they talking of, Phyllida wondered. Lieutenant Carter? Young Richard Morley? One of the harmless young men who had sent their dutiful posies. Well, their youthful flirtations could do no harm and would serve to keep Araminta out of mischief.

'I'm so pleased that you like him,' exclaimed Araminta. 'I think, no, I am sure, he feels something for me too! He is rather special, don't you think, Phyl?' she added shyly.

'I'm sure he's just perfect,' said Phyllida affectionately, smiling at Araminta's look of tender reminiscence. Yet it struck her with a pang too. So must she have looked after first meeting Ambrose. Perhaps one only ever looked like that with a first love, when all the world was changed and new. Later there were too many heartaches to be concealed.

Araminta embraced her cousin joyfully, picked up her flowers and left the room. It was now late, well after midday, but Phyllida sat on, quietly sipping her coffee. She had given instructions that she was not 'At Home' today: she did not think she could face the thought of Lord Hereward perhaps choosing to pay a call on Araminta and her having to chaperone her cousin while she saw him.

She was just contemplating ringing the bell for another cup of coffee, when the butler entered, bearing another bouquet of flowers.

'Oh! Miss Stukeley is gone upstairs, Carr.'

'These are for you, madam.'

Phyllida took them and thanked him. Whoever was it from? It was a posy of spring flowers, simply but tastefully done, and tied up with flowing yellow ribbons. It was set in a silver filigree posy holder. Phyllida breathed in the warm scent of the daffodils and primroses for a moment and then turned to open the note. It was very short and to the point.

Madam, she read, *I owe you an apology. I hope that you will allow me to deliver it in person. Yours. etc. FitzIvor.*

Phyllida stared at the letter. Lord Hereward wished to apologize. But why? She knew that he had misjudged her, but whatever had happened to make him change his mind in less than twelve hours? The butler, entering some ten minutes later, found Phyllida, her face delicately flushed, staring quite blindly into her empty coffee cup.

*　　*　　*

After his note, Phyllida half-expected Lord Hereward to pay a call on them that afternoon, and was ashamed to find her heart beating faster every time she heard footsteps on the stairs or voices in the hall. But he did not come. They did, however, have a call from Thorold, who came and spent a correct half-hour enquiring after the ladies' health. He looked more cheerful than usual, or at least less tongue-tied. He even (though Phyllida was sure unwittingly) contradicted Mrs Osborne.

Mrs Osborne had been most put out at the ball to overhear a remark about her 'carrot-haired granddaughter, Araminta Stukeley'. In spite of the fact that the lady who uttered these words had two plain daughters she had failed to dispose of in several unsuccessful seasons, and so need not be taken seriously, Mrs Osborne's wrath ran long—possibly because she had many times said the same thing. Phyllida's hair could be termed russet, or chestnut: Araminta's was plain, unadulterated red.

'Queen Boadicea had red hair, Tacitus tells us,' remarked Thorold.

'I have no opinion of Boadicea,' replied Mrs Osborne quellingly. 'A most unrespectable female.' Mrs Osborne infinitely preferred the Romans, who ran things with calm efficiency in an orderly fashion. If any of them had had red hair, she had never heard of it.

'But a heroine, surely, Mrs Osborne?'

'She was not the kind of female one would like to admit to one's drawing-room,' replied Mrs Osborne repressively.

Araminta glanced at Thorold, whose astonishment at this point of view was so marked that she had to turn away to stifle a giggle.

104

'Never mind, Grandmama,' said Phyllida, with a quelling glance at her cousin. 'Araminta danced every dance, and I am sure you had many more compliments on her looks than on the colour of her hair.'

'You are right, my dear Phyllida. Your remark is very just.' She then recollected that she had hopes of Phyllida and the Earl: she would leave the young people together for a while. When she had left (having sent her compliments to the Countess) Araminta could not contain herself and burst out laughing.

'It's just the picture of Boadicea sweeping into Grandmama's drawing-room!'

After a moment Thorold joined in. Poor Drusilla, he thought suddenly, so prim, so scared of life—so unable to laugh. Little Caroline laughed all the time: at the antics of the puppy on the lawn, or naughty giggles when she had hidden his pen behind the cushions. She was a poppet and he loved her dearly. He thought perhaps she might like Araminta.

The following morning Phyllida and Araminta had arranged to go riding. They went early, before the fashionables came out, at a time when, accompanied only by Danbury, Mrs Osborne's sober, middle-aged groom, they could enjoy a good gallop and startle only a few ducks rather than the stern Society matrons. Phyllida found that she missed the long, unchaperoned rambles in the country and she was pleased that Araminta's overflowing energy made her happy to accompany her.

Increasingly Phyllida found that she needed periods of quiet reflection which were not afforded her in the bustle of a London Season. In one way she was enjoying herself, of course she was. She had grown fond of Araminta and found her grandmother a source of quiet amusement, but she missed her dear papa and the countryside she knew. His weekly letters were unsatisfactory, dealing almost exclusively as they did, with the behaviour of his favourite moths or butterflies.

At home in the country, Phyllida felt that she was useful. There were villagers to be visited, jam to be made, bacon to be salted, all the thousand and one things to do to keep a home going on a small income. On the other hand, she was often bored there. The vicar's daughters, who might have been her friends, were interested only in hunting; the squire was an absentee landlord; there was nobody she could converse with on equal terms.

In London too much had happened too fast. She had had no time to absorb it all: the hostility from Lord Hereward and Mrs Gainford, Mr Marchmont positively haunting the house, Miss Lucy Telford sending her sentimental little notes. She had no time to allow these things to assume their proper place in her mind. And she felt useless. There were no duties towards those less fortunate than herself, nothing she had to do beyond decide which colour ribbons would best suit her new bonnet. Papa had written that he was sure London was doing her good—it was time she came out of her chrysalis a little. Phyllida was beginning to feel like one of the gaudy butterflies he had pinned on special glass-covered shelves in his study.

Now she found herself thinking about Ambrose. Lord Hereward (and Mrs Osborne too) had indicated that he was a good-for-nothing, a fortune-seeker and worse. Then Mrs Gainford had, in her haste to cover up, revealed that there were things about him she would prefer her daughter-in-law not to know.

All this was acutely painful to Phyllida. Ambrose had been her first love. Her life with him had been tragically brief. To have people depriving her of the pleasures of his memory was hard indeed. Yet, what was he doing in '14? Lord Hereward seemed to suggest that he was busy dissipating the fortune he had won from Taunton. How could anybody spend £10,000 in a year? It was the very sum that Mrs Osborne was proposing to settle on Phyllida herself, and she looked on that as providing a respectable income for the rest of her days. £500 a year would give her and Papa all the comforts of life and some of its elegancies. They might go to Italy for the winter, which she knew Papa had always wanted to do. How could Lord Hereward ever imagine that Ambrose had spent all that in so short a time?

Phyllida and Araminta had been in the park for about twenty minutes when suddenly there was a shout.

'By the living jingo! It's Mrs Ambrose!'

Phyllida turned. Two officers on horses were cantering towards them. Phyllida instantly recognized the facings on their jackets.

'Major Quentin,' she cried. 'And Captain Kaye!'

Greetings were exuberantly exchanged. Phyllida introduced them to Araminta, 'Major Quentin and Captain Kaye—my cousin, Miss Stukeley. From my husband's regiment, Araminta.'

Major Quentin wheeled his horse round to walk beside Phyllida. Captain Kaye, falling behind with Araminta, expressed the hope that he might see some more of her while he was on furlough.

Phyllida had always liked Major Quentin. He was rather older than Ambrose, in his forties, with greying hair and an impressive moustache. It was he who, in spite of the pressures of overwork and a leg wound, had found time to sit with Phyllida in her first shock of bereavement and arranged for her to visit her husband's grave, dispose of his effects and had sent his wife round to see if she needed any more help before embarking on the boat.

They talked for some time about mutual

108

acquaintances and then Phyllida said, somewhat hesitantly, 'I should like to ask you a question in confidence, if I may, Major.'

'Of course.' He glanced back over his shoulder. Captain Kaye and Araminta were now about fifteen yards behind them and out of ear-shot.

'Since I have been in London I have heard that Ambrose was involved in a gambling incident with a Mr Taunton, who subsequently killed himself. Ambrose won a large sum of money. Did you know about this?'

'Yes, I did,' replied Major Quentin in his open way. 'But, Mrs Ambrose, a man shouldn't gamble unless he has the wherewithal to pay, you know. It was in no way your husband's fault. Ambrose was reckless, but he played fair.'

'It is not that that is worrying me, Major. What happened *afterwards*?'

'His colonel ordered him to rusticate for a while: I believe he went to his parents. There was some talk of asking him to resign his commission, but he was a damned good officer and they were reluctant to lose him. Then this business with Prinny blew up.'

'What business with Prinny?'

'He didn't tell you? Glad to know the young hot-head could be discreet about something! Remember what was happening in '14, Mrs Ambrose. Fat old King Louis was leaving exile in London to go back to Paris. It was important that that went without a hitch. Our noble Prince had to be restrained somehow from following him—supposing Princess Caroline took it into her head to go too! Consider the political embarrassment if the Prince's estranged wife pursued him to Paris!

'Ambrose always was a favourite of Prinny's. It was decided by the powers-that-be that his part in an unsavoury scandal would be overlooked if he made himself useful in Brighton trying to restrain the Prince from going to France.'

'So he was in Brighton during most of that year?'

'Yes.' Major Quentin did not add that he had had the most glamorous actress in keeping for most of that time and had spent a small fortune on her.

'And the money he won?'

'My dear Mrs Ambrose. I fear that it probably went to enrich Prinny. He plays deep, you know. Life in Brighton can be very expensive.'

Phyllida thanked him and turned the conversation. The gentlemen escorted the cousins home and asked permission to call before they rejoined their regiment.

'We shall be delighted to see you both,' said Phyllida smiling. The officers bowed and turned to go. 'Oh, Major Quentin.' Phyllida ran down the steps and held out her hand. 'Thank you.'

*　　*　　*

Araminta, in the throes of first love—not to mention the heady excitements of a stolen adventure—was looking quite blooming. One night, alarmed and thrilled in about equal measure, she had tip-toed down to the kitchen armed with a feather (extracted with difficulty from her pillow) and taken some oil to anoint the back-door hinges. The kitchen with its black shadows and the embers of the fire glowing red looked agreeably scary and when the cat, yellow eyes glowing, gave a sudden 'miaow' and jumped off the range, Araminta squeaked and nearly dropped her candle.

She related all this with relish to Antony the next day when she met him by chance in Mudie's Circulating Library. Antony, though Araminta did not know it, was suffering all the inconveniences of a hangover. He had been drinking with some cronies into the small hours and Araminta's vivacity echoed inside his head like exploding rockets. He listened with half an ear and, as soon as the opportunity arose, pulled her round the bookshelves, wedged her firmly against the latest volumes by 'The Author of Waverley' and kissed her thoroughly. Anything to stop her talking! Araminta flung her arms round his neck and kissed him back with enthusiasm.

'Sweet girl,' said Antony, stroking her cheek. 'And a rash little one too! Supposing

111

somebody had seen us?'

'I wouldn't care!'

'Then I must care for you.' If anybody spilled the beans to Mrs Osborne, he thought, then I can say goodbye to £60,000. 'Discretion, Araminta! Now listen, we mustn't meet again until Wednesday evening. I shall have a cab waiting round the corner by the drinking fountain at nine o'clock.'

'I'll be there!' Araminta reached up and kissed him again, then whisked herself back round the corner to where Phyllida was getting out her chosen books.

Phyllida gave her books to the maid who was accompanying them and set off down Bond Street with Araminta, who stopped every now and then to exclaim over some object in a shop window.

'Oh, Phyl, silver lace! Would that go with my white evening dress, do you think?'

Phyllida was just about to answer when she heard herself being hailed.

'L ... Lord Hereward!' the colour flooded her cheeks.

'Mrs Gainford. Miss Stukeley.'

'Oh, hello, Lord Hereward,' said Araminta brightly. 'Will you excuse me if I just pop inside this shop to enquire about something? It's all right, Phyl. Hetty can come with me.' She disappeared inside the shop followed by the maid.

There was a moment's awkward pause.

112

Phyllida studied the York paving stones.

'Mrs Gainford,' began Hereward, 'I should like to talk to you sometime, maybe during the interval of the opera on Wednesday? But perhaps you do not wish to talk to me? If you don't, I assure you that I shall not annoy you by my presence.'

His voice was grave for once, the blue eyes serious. Phyllida raised her eyes to his and tried to calm her racing heart. 'I am conscious that my own behaviour that evening was too impetuous, my lord,' she said, tearing her eyes away from those blue depths with an effort. 'May we start again? Where things need to be discussed we might try to discuss them rationally.'

'You are very generous,' replied Hereward. 'I was grievously at fault, I know.' He held out his hand, 'May I look forward to our better acquaintance?'

Long after he had gone, Phyllida could still feel the warmth and strength of his fingers through the cotton of her gloves.

*   *   *

Emma Winter, bosom heaving, eyes flashing, stormed up and down her drawing-room, picked up a Sèvres figurine off her mantelpiece as she passed and flung it into the marble fireplace, where it exploded into pieces. Nell watched helplessly as the head of the little shepherdess shattered and one tiny porcelain hand fell on to the carpet and was ground under Emma's cork-tipped heel.

'Mrs Ambrose Gainford! Ha! If only she knew!'

'Knew what, Em?'

'Never you mind.' Emma kicked aside the remains of the shepherdess and threw herself down on the *chaise-longue*, pummelling the cushion in a pent-up fury. 'She'll regret it!'

'I don't see what you're getting so het up about, Em,' remarked Nell, wondering resentfully just how much the Sèvres figurine had cost. 'I thought his nibs was interested in t'other one, so Tony was saying. So what if he sent the widow some flowers? Honestly, I'd never have mentioned it if I'd known you would take it so hard.'

'I don't know what game your friend Tony's playing,' spat Emma, her grey eyes steely, 'but from now on this is my game, see? Let me think!'

'What's she like, Em?' ventured Nell after a moment. 'Old?'

'I don't know. I've never set eyes on the creature. Wait a minute, Nell.' Emma thought for a moment, her fingers drumming on the arm of the *chaise-longue*. Then she sat up and rang the bell. 'I want my carriage round,' she said, when the maid appeared. 'I'm going to pay a call!'

114

Mrs Gainford and Miss Amelia Heywood were sitting quietly in their morning-room, Mrs Gainford idly turning over the pages of *La Belle Assemblée*, and Amelia sewing some new ribbons on to Mrs Gainford's night cap, when the butler entered, bearing a card on a silver salver. From the distance at which he proffered the card it was plain that the visitor did not meet with his approval.

Mrs Gainford, suddenly pale, stared at the card, and with trembling fingers passed it to her cousin.

'Oh no!' gasped Amelia, 'it can't be.'

'You had better show her up,' said Mrs Gainford, pushing *La Belle Assemblée* behind a cushion and taking a volume of sermons on to her lap, as if its heavy tooled binding would render her impregnable. 'Amelia, stay here! I may need you.'

Some minutes later the door opened.

'Please enter, Miss Winter.' Mrs Gainford inclined her head slightly.

Emma undid the ribbons of her hat and sat down on the nearest chair, putting her large sealskin muff on to a small rosewood table next to her.

Mrs Gainford had not asked her to be seated and she cast a speaking glance at Amelia who was staring, taking in every detail of Emma's opulent (and expensive) appearance. 'What do

115

you want?' said Mrs Gainford at last in a less certain voice.

'Oh! I'm not here to make trouble,' smiled Emma, throwing open her pelisse and revealing, to Amelia's stunned fascination, a carriage dress of deep rose-pink silk, trimmed with silk floss and adorned with a splendid ruby and diamond pendant. 'I only want a little co-operation.'

She's obviously not short of a penny, thought Amelia resentfully. Her own well-armoured virtue had given her the paltry allowance of £50 a year and all the discomforts of being at her cousin's beck and call. The outcast Miss Winter was obviously worth twenty times that amount.

'Did you know that Mrs Ambrose Gainford was in Town?' asked Emma.

'I did.' Mrs Gainford spoke through stiffened lips.

'Have you seen her?'

'Briefly.'

'And what is she like?'

'About twenty-five, red hair, but well-enough, wouldn't you say, Amelia?'

'Her manners must please and her virtue is unquestionable,' replied Amelia with another envious glance at Emma.

A paragon, thought Emma savagely. 'Let me be frank, Mrs Gainford. I have no interest in the lady *unless* she becomes involved with Lord Hereward FitzIvor. *Then* I could make life very unpleasant indeed.'

'Do you have any expectation of it?' asked Mrs Gainford. 'A widow and not in her first youth. I am sure that you need have no apprehension.'

'I trust not, for all our sakes. Believe me, Mrs Gainford. I am prepared to go to any lengths.'

Amelia's agile mind had been working rapidly. Miss Winter meant what she said, she could see that, and she had the knowledge to ruin Augusta. Amelia dreaded to think what life would be like down at Avenell without the prospect of a London trip to escape from Mr Gainford's sulks and meannesses from time to time.

'Perhaps it should be made clear to Mrs Ambrose what Miss Winter's interest is in Lord Hereward,' she said. 'What do you think, Augusta?'

'An excellent idea,' broke in Emma cordially. 'I shall do myself the pleasure of seeing that she is fully informed. A virtuous young widow! What a shock to her sensibilities!'

'I think it would be better,' said Mrs Gainford slowly, 'if I broke the news to her myself.'

When Emma arrived home later that afternoon there was a folded note for her on the hall table. She picked it up. It was from Bridget, one of the housemaids in the Gifford house in St James's Square. Emma had long ago established a system of bribery with regard to Lord Hereward, for though during most of the year he usually spent the nights with her in Chelsea, whenever his brother or grandmother were in Town he based himself in St James's Square and she saw him much less often. If Lord Hereward had any plans for pensioning her off, she wanted to be acquainted with them well in advance. She opened the note.

Honoured Miss, she read. *Lord H. goes to the oprar on wedninsday. The erl and old lady goes with him and a lady Mrs Ganeford. Yr humble sarvint, Bridget Smalley.*

Emma twisted the note and held it up to the candle, turning it this way and that until it was quite consumed. The grey ash floated down and disappeared into the pattern on the carpet.

Very well then, she thought, if Hereward and Mrs Ambrose could go to the opera—so could she. Hm! The Duke of Knaresborough had a box directly opposite the Gifford box—and his lordship had once or twice shown himself more than ready to escort the beautiful Emma Winter!

'Polly?' she said some time later to her maid, 'is Harriet Clarke still with Knaresborough?'

'Yes, miss, I believe so.'

'Good, she owes me a favour.' The prim and virtuous Mrs Gainford was in for a very nasty surprise!

Later that evening a note in Miss Winter's handwriting arrived at Mrs Gainford's house.

Mrs Gainford read it and smiled.

*　　*　　*

Araminta need not have worried about Phyllida being suspicious, for Phyllida was far too taken up with her own concerns on Wednesday evening to wonder how her cousin was going to spend her time. True, she did ask, 'Shall you not be bored, Araminta? I am sure the Telford girls would be pleased to have you for the evening. Would you like me to send Hetty round with a note?'

'With those sad bores? No, thank you! Hetty can wash my hair for me and I shall have an early night, I think.' She yawned ostentatiously.

Phyllida dropped the subject. In truth, she would hardly have noticed if Araminta had announced her intention of going out with Antony Herriot, her mind revolved around one question only—whatever would Lord Hereward say to her?—and a second, more feminine preoccupation: what am I going to wear?

She decided on a new bronze-green silk with the scallop edging. It picked up both the highlights in her hair and the green of her eyes. When she came downstairs, shortly before seven, Mrs Osborne surveyed her with approval before she drove off to her card party.

'A very clever colour for you, my dear

Phyllida,' she pronounced in her majestic way. 'Most unusual. But for heaven's sake, remove that abominable cap!'

'But I am a widow, Grandmama!'

Mrs Osborne dismissed this as irrelevant. 'Your marriage lasted barely three months and you are but five-and-twenty, so we need not consider a cap.' Besides, she thought, to wear a cap practically proclaimed her as being on the shelf. Lord Gifford was diffident enough as it was, a widow's cap might put him off completely.

Somewhat to her surprise, Phyllida made no further protest.

'Good girl! If I win, you shall have some guineas to spend. Now, where's Araminta?'

'I believe Hetty is washing her hair.'

'Very well. Enjoy yourself, my dear. Fanny will wait up for you. You will say everything that is proper to the Countess, of course.'

Mrs Osborne left and Phyllida wandered into the drawing-room. The Gifford carriage was coming for her at seven o'clock. It now wanted but ten minutes to the hour. Phyllida paced agitatedly up and down the Aubusson carpet and tried to quell the jumping of her heart. Of course she was right to be a *little* nervous, she told herself sternly. Anything more was quite out of place. She was a widow, twenty-five, mature, and past the age of childish nerves. She would be sober, cool, calm.

Why then did her heart insist on beating so fast?

Araminta had summoned Hetty to wash her hair at six o'clock and now sat in front of her bedroom fire rubbing it dry with a towel and brushing vigorously. The fire made her red hair glow until it seemed that her waves and curls were a reflection of the leaping flames in the grate.

Araminta's bedroom was large and cosy and held, besides her tent bed and pretty chintz-covered dressing-table, an old, worn sofa, a cheval looking-glass and shelves full of her old toys and dolls, for she had had the room since her parents had died and it contained all the motley remnants of childhood. When she was little, she infinitely preferred it to the chilly schoolroom, and often had her supper here. Tonight she did the same, snuggling up on the sofa, a rug over her feet, a worn woolly rabbit at her back and a tray on a small table by her.

When she heard her grandmother go out she got up and went to the window to look. Yes, there she was, two tall ostrich plumes causing her almost to bend double to get into the carriage. Araminta mentally ticked one off and sat down to wait. At seven o'clock she heard the Gifford carriage and again watched discreetly from behind her flowered curtains as Phyllida climbed in and was driven off to St James's Square.

Araminta rang the bell for Hetty.

'Here's the tray, Hetty. I shan't need you again tonight.'

'Are you sure, miss?' But Hetty was relieved. Her young man came round on Wednesdays when Mrs Osborne was out and she wanted the chance of a quiet kiss and cuddle without the bell summoning her all the time.

Araminta yawned. 'Yes. I'm sleepy. I might go to bed early.'

'Very well, miss. Good-night.'

'Good-night, Hetty.'

Two hours to go! As soon as Hetty had clattered downstairs, Araminta went to her wardrobe and took out one of her old schoolgirl cotton frocks. It would have been lovely to amaze Tony with her new celestial-blue spotted muslin, but Araminta had had enough experience of stolen outings to know that she must not be recognized. A schoolgirl's dress it would have to be rather than the unmistakable raiment of the débutante.

She tied her hair into a tight braid and pulled out an old drab-coloured cloak from her wardrobe. It had a large hood and would hide that tell-tale hair! After some thought she slipped a few shillings into her pocket, together with her handkerchief and a piece of string. Then she took her bolster, pushed it down her bed and rumpled up the blankets. There! From a distance and in the half-light of the fire, it looked like a sleeping form. She tucked the woolly rabbit in beside it and picked up her cloak. Nearly nine and yes! there was a closed hackney carriage just turning the corner.

Araminta slipped downstairs, silently unlocked the back-door, locked it behind her and threaded the key on a string round her neck, where it hung cold and heavy.

She could see the shadows of the servants in the basement as she went past and turned the corner. And there was Antony!

CHAPTER FIVE

Lady Gifford paused on the steps leading up to the Opera House, Covent Garden, one gnarled hand resting on Hereward's arm, the other gripping an ebony walking cane, and turned to look where Phyllida was descending from the carriage and taking Thorold's proffered arm. Cecilia Osborne was right, she thought, Thorold and Mrs Gainford would be very well suited. If the *ton* noticed his attentions tonight, they would also notice that she was well content, and that would still any malicious tongues, ready to make mischief.

It was a pity about the Gainford connection, but she did not doubt her ability to deal a severe snub to Augusta Gainford should she become encroaching. But there was nothing wrong with Phyllida's breeding: the Danbys were a good enough county family, and the

Osbornes fit to mate where they would. Phyllida herself was attractive, intelligent and her manners were above reproach: she would do very well for Thorold.

Phyllida, hemmed in by the crush of people going upstairs inside the Opera House, stood halfway up the stairs and looked down into the foyer. It was crowded and the hundreds of candles sparkled off necklaces and tiaras, for the cream of the upper 10,000 were here tonight. (Little did she know it, but the flower of the *demi-monde* were also here, their languishing eyes and saucy innuendoes sending outraged shivers through the respectable bosoms of Society matrons with daughters to dispose of.)

Phyllida looked about her with shining eyes: how beautiful it all was! The brilliance of the ladies' jewellery, the silks and laces of their dresses, were all set off by the sober black and white of the gentlemen. None, to her wondering eyes, was more brilliant than a voluptuous lady, with hair so black that it shone like jet, wearing a diaphanous dress cut low over her magnificent breasts and revealing, in every sinuous line, far more of the wearer's charms than was strictly seemly.

Had she seen her before, Phyllida did not remember, but it was plain that everybody knew very well who she was, for she could see several ladies of her acquaintance looking at the lady and whispering behind their fans.

How wonderful to be so very lovely, Phyllida thought wistfully: to embody the silly schoolgirl's dream of being able to turn every male head simply by walking into the room.

The crowd of people now moved forward and Phyllida turned and followed Lady Gifford up the red carpeted stairs towards their box. As she turned she caught sight of her mother-in-law with her depressed cousin Amelia down in the foyer and, catching her eye, bowed politely. Mrs Gainford inclined her head graciously and raised one languid hand.

The Gifford box was positioned more for the occupants to see their friends opposite than to see the stage. Lady Gifford, seated with Phyllida beside her, greeted all her old acquaintances, smiling and nodding at some and peering at others through her lorgnette. It was with reluctance that she turned her attention to the stage when, at the end of the overture, the curtain rose.

The opera, *Penelope* by Domenico Cimarosa, opened to a scene of moonlight, bathing a variety of fallen classical columns in a greeny-blue light. Phyllida saw from her programme that the young soprano, Signorina Guiditta Pasta, was making her first appearance on the London stage. Indeed, so many were the broken capitals, pediments and bits of fallen masonry littering the stage, it was at first problematical whether Signorina Pasta would be able to negotiate these hazards successfully and appear on the stage at all. She was small and slightly built, with liquid dark eyes, but her voice, though clear and sweet, was not powerful and, at times, was almost drowned out by the orchestra. Phyllida noticed, however, that several gentlemen had their eye-glasses raised, the better to appreciate the signorina's charms.

Phyllida sat back in her chair and happily lost herself in the music.

Thorold, sitting behind Phyllida, shut his eyes and tried to quieten his growing physical discomfort. He was always affected by smoky candles and dust, and now he felt the familiar smarting of his eyes and his breathing became tighter. As a child he had been subject to crippling attacks of asthma, and the resulting quiet régime imposed by his mother had strengthened his diffidence and his turn for scholarship. Now he had largely grown out of the asthma, but he still avoided a close, smoke-filled atmosphere whenever he could.

As the first act closed and the curtain fell Thorold realized he would have to leave.

'I'm sorry, Grandmama,' he wheezed, 'but you know how it is.'

'Oh dear! Thorold! Shall you be all right?'

'Yes! Yes! A breath of fresh air is all I need. Don't worry about me.'

Phyllida expressed her concern.

'Please do not worry, Mrs Gainford. I shall be as right as rain in the morning. I am only

126

sorry to break up the party. But my brother will look after you.'

As Thorold left, the doors of their box opened and Sir Marmaduke and Lady Vavasour entered to greet Lady Gifford. Phyllida was introduced and subjected to Sir Marmaduke's searching gaze and a 'Mrs Ambrose Gainford. Well, well.' She said a few words and then retreated tactfully to the back of the box.

'Mrs Gainford,' said Hereward quietly, 'I happen to know that Floyds' box is empty. Shall we go there?'

Phyllida allowed herself to be led out and along the corridor. They sat down in the shadow at the back of the box. Hereward sat, head bowed for a moment, as if he was carrying a burden too great to bear and then said, 'I should like to be open with you, Mrs Gainford. May I be assured of your discretion?'

'Certainly, my lord.' Phyllida had never heard Hereward speak so seriously.

'Sir Marmaduke, you may know, occupied a very high position in the War Office, and he told me, in confidence, that there was enough evidence to believe that Johnny Taunton was spying for the French. Apparently, his involvement was a way of paying off debts he had incurred while at Oxford.'

'I am sorry, my lord,' said Phyllida gently. 'Sir Marmaduke's revelation must have been a blow to you.'

'Thank you, Mrs Gainford. You are kinder to me than I deserve after what I said to you that evening. It is not you but I who must carry some responsibility for poor Johnny's death, and that I find hard to bear.'

'What responsibility is that?' asked Phyllida puzzled.

'Only the heedlessness of youth,' replied Hereward with a bitter smile. 'I was wealthy, Johnny was not. Oxford was expensive. I knew it and yet I cannot, to my shame, think of even one occasion where I curtailed my own extravagant activities to accommodate Johnny's slender purse—or even considered doing so. And yet I called myself his friend!'

'My lord, do not take it so to heart! Think, would you, had your positions been reversed, have sold information to the French?'

'Good God, no!'

'You cannot take on the responsibility for the weaknesses of another human being, my lord, only for yourself. I do not doubt that you were generous to your friend in other ways.'

Hereward shrugged. 'Johnny came to stay frequently at Maynard. I put him up for White's when he came to London. But those were easy things to do. I never *listened* to him, Mrs Gainford, that is what I regret now.'

'Nevertheless,' Phyllida observed with a smile, 'you have learned from that. You have agreed to listen to me!'

Hereward laughed, his voice lightened.

'Only after one bungled effort!'

'Even so. But perhaps you will allow me to say what *I* have learned, Lord Hereward, since I saw you last. I met an old friend, Major Quentin, on furlough from my husband's regiment and asked him about this sad affair. He told me that Ambrose was in Brighton for most of '14. It appears that he was a pet of the Prince Regent, and the War Office thought he would be usefully employed amusing the Prince and taking his mind off any thoughts of following King Louis to Paris.'

'So they agreed to overlook his part in an unsavoury scandal, is that it?'

'So it would appear.'

'I suppose there is no need to enquire then what happened to the money?' It would be thrown down on the gaming table, every last penny of it, thought Hereward. Gainford was fortunate to have got off so lightly. Even if he had won at Prinny's table it would be doubtful if he would have been paid. Mrs Gainford was luckier than she knew in losing her husband so conveniently when she did.

But Johnny's death? Had Gainford been implicated in that? Or had the political convenience of the suicide been entirely coincidental? He could not ask her. Whatever Gainford had or had not done, he could see now that Phyllida was innocent. She was a lovely and honest girl and he liked her too much to cause her needless distress. How

129

different from Emma, whose beauty hid a mercenary and calculating deviousness.

For the first time in his life Hereward found himself feeling unsure. What did Phyllida think of him now? She had spoken kindly, but was that mere politeness or had she genuinely forgiven his rudeness? Suddenly, more than anything in the world, Hereward wanted her liking and respect—and never did he feel less confident of having it.

From her seat in the box opposite, Emma Winter raked the auditorium with steely eyes looking for her quarry.

*   *   *

The Vauxhall Pleasure Gardens juggler, a swarthy Indian with curly black hair, dressed in a yellow leotard covered with spangles, set his plates spinning through the air, like so many whirling moons. It was now half past nine, and dark, but the thousands of fairy lights strung along the wrought-iron tracery of the pavilions lit the scene with a sparkling brilliance, and Araminta clapped her hands in delight.

'Oh, Antony!' she cried, 'this is far, far better than the Bath circus. Ooo, look at that dear little dancing dog. Do let us go and see!'

Antony was an habitué of the Vauxhall Pleasure Gardens, but usually he paid very little attention to its sundry attractions,

130

preferring to steer his chosen companion as swiftly as possible down the Dark Walk to some secluded grotto. Araminta was laughing as the dog, wearing a blue jacket with a frill round the neck, cavorted about on its hind legs, jumped through hoops and finally trotted round the circle of onlookers with a collecting bag round its neck, begging for pennies.

'Here!' said Antony, handing Araminta some pennies. The little dog sat up and begged in front of her and then barked to show its appreciation.

Antony looked at the dog with dislike. A cheap circus trick! Suitable only for schoolchildren and hobbledehoys. He had every intention of persuading Araminta that a little walk down one of the unfrequented paths was what she wanted, and was bored by her interest in the side-shows. However it wouldn't do to rush her. He moved behind her and put his arms around her waist, pulling her back against him and began to nuzzle her neck gently.

'Antony!' Araminta spoke in a breathless voice.

'Only a little cuddle,' said Antony caressingly. 'Look, everybody's doing it!'

'Oh!' Araminta jumped. 'What was that?'

'Only the cannon.'

A loudhailer came across the air. 'Ladies and gentlemen! The grand representation of the Battle of Waterloo will commence in five

131

minutes. One thousand men! Two hundred horses! The entire glorious action staged before your very eyes! Hurry! Hurry! Ladies and gentlemen! The Battle of Waterloo commences in five minutes.'

'Quickly, Antony, or we shall be late!'

'You don't want to see that, Araminta,' said Antony impatiently. 'It's not worth it, I give you my word. Come, let us go somewhere quiet.'

'But I want to see it!'

'And I want to be with you.'

Araminta pushed his arms away impatiently. 'You will be with me,' she said pettishly. 'Oh, please, Antony. Please let us see the Battle of Waterloo! It sounds such fun!'

'Tell you what,' said Antony cunningly. 'Let's go this way. It's the long way round but we end up on a slight rise: you'll be able to see better from there.'

'All right, come along.' Araminta eagerly pulled Antony down the long and lonely path he had indicated.

*   *   *

Thorold stood outside the Opera House and leaned against one of the pillars of the portico, breathing deeply. The cool night air held a smell of vegetables and rotting flowers from the market nearby, but Thorold breathed in gratefully, feeling his chest becoming less tight.

132

Once or twice some hopeful nocturne accosted him with a 'Good evening, sir. Not a pleasant evening to be on your own. Like a bit of company?'

Thorold waved them away and looked up at the star-studded sky, for it was a clear night with only a few dark blue clouds. The moon now sailed out from behind one. Thorold sighed. He remembered Caroline just before he came down to London, catching sight of the moon through the window of her night-nursery and holding out her little arms to the lovely bright yellow ball and crying, 'Want! Want!'

He missed his little daughter. He knew his grandmother had hoped for a grandson to secure the line, but Thorold wouldn't have traded Caroline for all the sons in the kingdom. Well, he couldn't get Caroline the moon to play with, but what she would like, he decided suddenly, would be a lot of little toys, the kind that everybody else would turn up their noses at. The sort of toys that only cost a penny or two that she could hold in her hand—not a big, expensive rocking horse she couldn't climb on to without assistance. What should he get? A monkey on a stick? A mouse on wheels? What would amuse her most?

All at once it seemed imperative that he get them immediately. Caroline might forget who he was, forget her Papa: he had been away for too long for her tender years. He could send the toys in the vegetable hamper that arrived from Maynard every Thursday and returned that evening. Now, where could he get what he wanted at this time of night? Ah, yes! He took a few steps forward and shouted, 'Cab!'

'Yes, sir! Where to, sir?'

'Vauxhall. The gardens.'

*   *   *

Phyllida sat through the second act of *Penelope* in a tumult of emotions. Somehow, she did not know how, while she had been sitting talking to Hereward, everything had altered. It was as if the entire balance of her life had changed, tipped gently over and she had fallen into a new dimension: a dimension where colours were brighter, feelings nearer the surface. All she could say with any clarity was that with him she felt more herself than she had ever been and at the same time, somebody quite other.

She had fallen head over heels in love.

Phyllida was no silly girl to be moonstruck by some handsome face, she was a mature woman, with enough heartbreak behind her to know that this time, it was very serious. She had fallen in love with Ambrose with all the ardour of an inexperienced heart and had taken no thought for the future. Now she looked into herself and knew that she had met her fate. At twenty-five one did not love lightly, nor go into something with eyes dazed by a rosy glow.

Hereward, she knew, was arrogant and a spoilt darling of Society. Countless women had set traps for him. Mamas had angled to get him to their daughters' dances, just as Lady Telford had done: the daughters had languished for a glance from those blue eyes. Everything in Phyllida revolted at the thought of joining their ranks. She knew now that he was generous and capable of dealing truthfully with both her and a distressing piece of his past: she would not abuse that in any way. If he wished to seek her out he would do so. She would not make herself the butt of every cruel wit by wearing her heart on her sleeve.

Having made this laudable resolve, Phyllida promptly broke it by replying, when Hereward leaned forward during a scene change and asked her what she thought of Ulysses, far more warmly than she meant. 'I'm surprised Nausicaa didn't mistake him for a beached whale!'

'He is certainly large enough,' laughed Hereward, his eyes warm and amused, and Phyllida could not stop herself smiling back. Their eyes held, blue into green, Phyllida's doubtful and Hereward's wary.

Then, in the darkness of the box, he reached forward and took her hand, undid the little buttons on her glove, and gently kissed her palm, folding her fingers round the kiss before putting her hand back into her lap.

When Lady Gifford turned to say something to Hereward and he answered her at random, Phyllida smiled down at her ungloved hand and looked at her palm, lost in a happy dream.

Then the doubts began to creep in. Perhaps he behaved like this to all the ladies? Phyllida, living as she had done in rural isolation, had not been the object of much gallantry before. Was that all it was? A little flirtation to while away the time? That contact, those feelings, so precious to her, might not have struck an answering chord in him. She did not know him very well, after all. Was she so green that she could fall in love on the strength of one short conversation and a kiss on the hand?

Men behaved differently over these things, she must remember that. She had seen a laughing Ambrose dispensing kisses to the barmaid before their embarkation at Dover; he had given a parting squeeze to the pretty Belgian chambermaid in Brussels. He had eyed attractive women down the length of the street. Yet these activities had meant very little, she knew. Phyllida could not imagine herself greeting the inn-keeper or footman with such familiarity. Was it so with Hereward? She was no chambermaid, it was true, but he may have meant less by it than her eager heart hoped for.

The second act drew to a close and Phyllida realized that she had not taken in a note of it.

'I thought the old nurse gave a very affecting performance, did you not think so, Mrs

Gainford?' asked Lady Gifford.

'Oh! Yes, indeed. Most moving,' replied Phyllida, hoping she'd got it right.

'What did you think, Hereward?'

'I'm sorry, Grandmama, I'm afraid I wasn't attending.'

'They must have been very absorbing thoughts then,' said Lady Gifford tartly.

'They were,' said Hereward soberly, and looked at Phyllida.

Suddenly there was a movement from the box opposite. The lady whom Phyllida had admired in the foyer had stood up and was waving at her. At *her*? Phyllida looked at Lady Gifford who had not noticed, being too busy greeting an elderly admirer who had entered the box. She looked round at Hereward. He was looking at the lady his eyes blazing like sapphires.

'Excuse me, Mrs Gainford,' he said, his face impassive, 'I have something I must see to.' He rose and left the box.

Before Phyllida could collect herself Mrs Gainford and Miss Heywood entered and she must pull herself together somehow and introduce them to Lady Gifford. Lady Gifford had never cared for what she had heard about Mrs Gainford and now she met her with her die-away airs, her dislike was confirmed. She therefore agreed to her admirer's suggestion that they take a little stroll, and left Phyllida alone with her mother-in-law.

Mrs Gainford sat down in Lady Gifford's vacated seat at the front of the box. Phyllida endeavoured to calm herself and began to enquire after her mama-in-law's health and whether she was enjoying the opera. Mrs Gainford answered briefly and the conversation lapsed.

Why has she come, thought Phyllida, if she has nothing to say to me?

Phyllida's manners had led her not to look around the theatre to see if she could see Lord Hereward, but Mrs Gainford had no such inhibitions. She was leaning forward scrutinizing the boxes opposite through her lorgnette and now she spoke. 'Well, I declare! That must be Lord Hereward, of course?'

Phyllida looked. Hereward had just entered the box and was bending over talking to the lady who had attracted their attention earlier. Phyllida could not help thinking how the gold of his hair perfectly complemented her raven curls.

'Yes, that is Lord Hereward,' she answered in a voice from which all emotion had been banished.

'I thought he would not be able to keep away,' said Mrs Gainford next, in a triumphant voice. 'What man would with so beautiful a creature?'

'I ... I do not know the lady.'

'Lady! Well!' Mrs Gainford laughed. 'No, my dear, that is Emma Winter, once darling of the stage and now Lord Hereward's mistress!'

'His mistress!' Phyllida could only echo.

'Yes, I understand they have been together for several years now. They are quite devoted!'

* * *

'Let me go, oh, please let me go!' whispered Araminta, her voice trembling in a pathetic break.

'Come, little love, I won't hurt you! What are you so frightened of?'

'It's late ... I didn't realize...' stammered Araminta, quite as much confused by Antony's feelings as her own. Once, in the safety of her own room, it had seemed like all she had ever wanted, to be alone with Antony in a secluded place, welcoming his caresses, and far from the prying eyes of chaperones. Now, she was frightened. Antony was holding her too close, touching her in a way that somehow shamed her. She loved him, of course she did, but just now all she wanted was to find herself safely at home.

'Delicious little prude,' said Antony appreciatively, fingering the buttons on her bodice.

'No ... no!' pleaded Araminta.

'Come on, you'll like it, I promise you!'

But the more she squirmed the more excited he became. All at once she remembered some advice Belinda's escort had given them on one of their stolen excursions from the seminary. She went limp, Antony relaxed his hold, and Araminta, in one swift, unladylike movement, brought up her knee sharply. Antony doubled up and Araminta fled.

She did not stop running until she reached the shouts and smoke from the re-enactment of the battle of Waterloo, and plunged, her heart still beating, into the crowd. Wedged in between several solid citizens and a fat woman with two grizzling children, Araminta could see little. But at least she was safe. Somewhere in front of her the battle raged; she could hear the whinnying of the horses and the shouts of the men. Occasionally there was a dull roar as the cannons fired and the air crackled with the sound of gun-shot.

The battle was nearing its climax now. A wooden replica of a French redoubt was about to go up in flames. She could see men swarming all over it above the heads of the crowd. Araminta forgot her fears and held her breath, her hands clasped in front of her. She did not notice a slim hand reach experimentally inside her pocket and extract the few coins.

'Look! Look! It's going!' cried a stout man behind her.

There was a sudden explosion which lit up the sky and then the whole structure shot up in flames. Rockets fired into the air, sending down showers of white sparks.

Araminta clapped her hands. How exciting!

How she wished she'd been there!

All at once there was the scream of an agonized horse and pandemonium broke out. A badly-aimed rocket had gone into one of the horse's eyes and its rider could not control it as it lashed out and tried to break free of the maddening pain. Its panic infected the other horses. Some broke free and the crowd scattered.

There were cries as mothers lost their children and people were trampled underfoot in the rush to escape. Araminta found herself swept along in the stampede, barely able to keep her footing. She pushed behind a hefty man as a horse plunged past, its eyes rolling with terror.

At last she found herself in one of the main alleyways that led to the pavilions and clung on to one of the wrought-iron lamp-posts as the crowd surged past and eventually left her, clinging there like a bit of flotsam on the shore after a storm.

Panting she felt for her key. It was there! Then her pocket. It was empty.

* * *

Thorold had entered the Pleasure Gardens some time earlier and had made his purchases in the quiet of the almost deserted arcades. There was an old peddler with a box around his neck selling little tin toys for a penny and

141

Thorold bought a selection of these: a brightly coloured parrot that swung on a perch, a little dog that beat a drum when you wound the handle, and some others. Then he went in search of a sugar-mouse stall. He heard the noise from the crowd, but it wasn't until the sugar-mouse man, looking over his shoulder said, 'My Gawd!' and ran, leaving Thorold holding a pink and green mouse, that he realized that something was wrong.

Suddenly, a horse broke through the crowd, one eye running blood, and plunged into the trees behind the pavilions, knocking over a gingerbread stall, its flying hooves narrowly missing a child crouching behind it. Thorold took one look at the crowd and did much as Araminta had done: vaulted over a wrought-iron barrier and braced himself against a pillar.

The crowd was pushing and straining to get out of the narrow entrance gates, and after a moment's thought Thorold decided that he'd be safest back towards where the battle had been fought. Eventually the gate would clear, but until then he would not risk life and limb trying to get out.

He set off down one of the paths when he was arrested by the sight of a woebegone little figure sobbing by a lamp-post. For a moment Thorold's heart stood still, then he shook himself. No, it couldn't be!

The figure straightened, the hood fell back, and there was the unmistakable glint of

142

copper curls.

'M ... Miss Stukeley!'

Araminta looked up, 'L ... Lord Gifford!' she said incredulously. Then, 'Oh, Lord Gifford!' She ran forward and flung herself into his arms.

Thorold patted her awkwardly on the shoulder and then sneezed, for her curls were tickling his nose.

'Come and sit down, Miss Stukeley,' he said indicating a bench. But it was plain that Araminta couldn't walk. Thorold picked her up as though she were Caroline and sat down with her on his knee, smoothing her hair and murmuring reassuring noises into her ear.

Eventually Araminta sat up. Thorold gave her his handkerchief and she blew her nose firmly and wiped her eyes.

'Good heavens,' she said, looking at his greatcoat pocket in amazement, for one side had torn, 'you've got a sugar mouse in there!'

'Yes,' said Thorold. 'Would you like it?' It somehow seemed appropriate that he give it to Araminta. 'I bought it for Caroline, but it seems to have lost its tail.'

'Thank you.' Araminta made no attempt to get down from his knee. Indeed she hardly seemed to realize that she was in such a compromising position. She leaned back contentedly against Thorold's shoulder, nibbled the sugar mouse and gave a sigh as if she had come home.

'You'd better tell me all about it,' said Thorold at last.

'Well, I will. Because you haven't scolded me. Only you will promise not to tell, won't you?'

'We'll see,' said Thorold diplomatically. 'I won't say anything to upset your grandmother if I can help it.'

Araminta told him, glossing over the name of her companion and saying only that she had lost him in the panic. She added that she had the key and could easily get in if she could get home: which she would have been able to do if she hadn't stupidly lost her money. Her tone of voice said very firmly that she was quite able to look after herself, thank you.

Thorold found her naïvety both endearing and hair-raising, but he made no comment on her story, only saying simply, 'I expect your money was stolen by a pick-pocket. Always plenty of those in a crowd. Could happen to anybody. Anyway, I think the best thing is for us to get a cab, don't you? I'll drop you near home and watch to make sure you get in safely.'

'Oh, thank you!' cried Araminta. She stood up and pulled her cloak up over her hair. 'The crowds have thinned out now. We should be all right, I think.'

'Come then.' Thorold offered her his arm.

It wasn't until they were in the cab that Araminta thought to ask Thorold what he was

144

doing at Vauxhall. Thorold showed her the little toys he had bought, holding them up to the window so that she could see them in the flare of the street lights as they passed.

Araminta was silent for a moment, then she burst out, 'Why do you allow everybody to think you are so sober and bookish, when you are not at all?'

'I'm a very dull chap, really,' said Thorold awkwardly.

'But that's not true! And I shan't allow anybody to say that ever again!' expostulated Araminta. He was quite, quite different, only the exciting bit was underneath and it didn't show.

*   *   *

Hereward did not know why he felt so murderous towards Emma. There was nothing he could accuse her of. He knew perfectly well that her intentions towards that lecherous goat, Knaresborough, whose box she was in, were quite platonic. The noble Duke was slatternly in the extreme; he smelt, his linen was spotted with grease and his fingernails encrusted with dirt. Moreover, he had a mistress in keeping who was friends, of a sort, with Emma. There was no reason why she should not have attended the opera if she wished, or, once there, not have greeted him across the auditorium.

145

Nevertheless, Hereward had felt an impulse to disown her. What Society thought of him mounting a mistress was not a question that had previously concerned him. He supposed that his grandmother knew, but she had never seen fit to discuss it with him and he had never raised the subject. But there was something about Phyllida's perfectly friendly but slightly aloof smile that greeted him on his return that made him wish passionately that Emma had not been there.

'I am so sorry, Mrs Gainford,' he said as he sat down, 'I had hoped to continue our conversation during this interval.'

'Not at all, my lord,' replied Phyllida calmly. 'More intimate acquaintances must take precedence, I believe.'

Hereward could hardly deny this statement—nor that Emma was indeed an intimate acquitance. He could find nothing to say that would express the tangled thoughts within him. For the first time in his life he was relieved when his grandmother returned and filled the silence by asking Phyllida how she had found her mama-in-law.

'Very well, thank you, ma'am.'

Lady Gifford looked at her guest critically. Phyllida was looking strained and white. It must have been that tiresome woman, Augusta Gainford, she thought, for the girl had been looking quite blooming before. Indeed, Lady Gifford had found herself lamenting Thorold's

146

absence, for surely he would succumb to so charming a creature?

'Come my dear,' she said kindly, 'tell me what is to happen in the third act.'

Emma, who made no pretence of any interest in the opera, and indeed found the warbling of Signorina Guiditta Pasta quite ridiculous, watched Phyllida during the third act from behind the shelter of her fan. Good! She noticed that Phyllida's eyes often glanced her way and that she seemed abstracted. Mrs Gainford had done her work well! Emma posed herself seductively, one white arm along the plush velvet of the box, and allowed the diamond bracelet Hereward had given her to twinkle in the candlelight, as she waved her hand gently in time to the music. Phyllida Gainford should see that it was she, Emma, Hereward wanted, not her.

Phyllida did see—very clearly. Mrs Gainford had taken care to inform her that all Emma's jewellery came from Hereward. 'So generous!' she had sighed. Emma's low-cut evening dress with its lace train had plainly been made by a first-class modiste. Phyllida had nothing but a locket which had belonged to her mother and she felt her dowdiness beside Emma's brilliance.

Her moment of reciprocated feeling with Hereward had been brief indeed. Now it was over. She trusted that he viewed her more sympathetically than before, but any other hopes she might have allowed herself must be quelled. She would chaperone Araminta to the best of her ability this Season, and then she would return home to look after Papa.

But somehow the attraction of this plan for herself had vanished. Phyllida loved her father and her Gloucestershire home, but the thought of living out the rest of her days there, looking after Papa, involving herself in the village concerns, now filled her with a sense of desolation.

Unknowingly, since she had come to London, Phyllida had been putting aside her past and, whether she was fully aware of it or not, was looking for a different future.

*   *   *

The opera ended. The ladies collected their reticules, programmes, fans and gloves and Hereward helped first his grandmother and then Phyllida on with their cloaks. They were to drop Phyllida home in their carriage before going on to St James's Square.

Phyllida pulled a number of polite nothings out of somewhere during the journey home and said everything that was proper in thanking their hostess. She could not look at Hereward.

'You're a good girl,' said Lady Gifford, patting her hand. 'I'm sure that my grandsons will be calling to see how you go on. I'm only sorry that Thorold could not have been with us.'

Phyllida sent her best wishes for Lord Gifford's recovered health.

Hereward saw her to the door but said little. His face, when Phyllida glanced up at him, seemed unusually stern in the moonlight. Perhaps he is bored and longing to get back to his cosy love-nest, thought Phyllida hopelessly. But he smiled as he bade her good-night and waited until the butler had opened the door before going back to the carriage. The carriage light caught the gold of his hair as he climbed in. Then the door shut and he was gone. Phyllida swallowed the lump in her throat and resolutely turned to go indoors.

'Charming girl,' said Lady Gifford, as the carriage set off again for St James's Square. 'I am quite determined that she and Thorold should make a match of it!'

'What!'

'Oh, you're thinking of the Gainford connection. I assure you that I shan't regard it. The girl has *quality*, Hereward. Thorold must see it.'

'Does ... does she care for him?'

'She likes him, certainly. Now I shall want your help in this, Hereward. Thorold will visit if you accompany him, where he may not venture on his own. You know how retiring he is! It is of the first importance that Thorold re-marries and has an heir and I have quite decided—and so incidentally has Cecilia Osborne—that Phyllida Gainford will suit him very well.'

Hereward's already tangled thoughts reeled under this new blow. His ravelled emotions were in disarray, but one thing was clear: Thorold must not marry Phyllida.

CHAPTER SIX

Antony, in a red brocade dressing-gown, picked up his post, surveyed it briefly and threw it down on the table. Tradesmen's bills! Was there no end to them? His luck at the faro tables had been quite out this week and were it not for a fortunate win at the cock-fighting down at Bunhill Fields he would be quite out-at-elbow.

He was also annoyed with Araminta. Whyever did the stupid chit agree to go down a darkened walk with him if she was then going to behave as though she was being molested? He had every reason to think that she was perfectly willing. Antony never considered anybody but himself for long, and if it crossed his mind that he'd betrayed Araminta's trust in him, he was easily able to dismiss it: a minx like that must know what's what.

However, she had £60,000, so any question of teaching her a lesson would have to wait. He would play the contrite lover for a while.

Antony arrived at the Osborne house, some hours later, complete with roses, just in time to see the Gifford carriage depositing Thorold and Hereward on the doorstep. Antony hesitated, then took a noiseless step or two back until he was standing in the shadow of a doorway. From there he watched, cold-eyed, as Thorold and Hereward knocked and were admitted.

Antony looked at the roses in his hand and thought furiously: he must put a stop to that at all costs! Until that unfortunate episode last night, Araminta had been quite spoony about him. But with her stupid over-reaction, not to mention the encouragement of friends and the envy of society, if Lord Hereward demonstrated an interest, she would soon be quite lost to him. He would have to move fast.

He pulled out his pocket book and consulted it. *Emma Winter* he had jotted down, after his visit to Nell, *Cheyne Walk*. Hm, no harm giving it a try.

Emma, wearing a charming morning-dress of embroidered clear lawn with a cherry-coloured sash, had just left her breakfast-table when Polly, her eyes popping with curiosity, brought in a card. Emma picked it up, raising her eyebrows as she read the inscription. 'How intriguing,' she said lightly. 'Show him into the drawing-room, Polly. I'll be with him in a few moments.'

Doubtless the gentleman was up to no good—but why not? Hereward had not been too pleased to see her last night at the opera, so why should she not amuse herself elsewhere? Did he expect her to live like a nun?

The gentleman could cool his heels for a while—she would go and change.

'Mr Herriot!' said Emma brightly, some half an hour later. 'How good of you to call.'

Antony offered her the flowers and bowed, one hand on his heart.

Emma laughed and thanked him. 'To what do I owe the pleasure of this visit?'

'We have a mutual interest,' Antony reminded her. Emma was pleasurably aware as his appraising eyes travelled over her, that his words had more than one meaning. She allowed her own eyes to wander approvingly. But Antony was continuing, 'I want a certain noble lord to keep away from a certain young lady. This morning I saw the same noble lord, with his owlish brother, paying a call on the lady in question.'

'Oh?' Emma frowned. A courtesy call, no doubt, but all the same.

'So I thought perhaps that you and I might see what might be done about it. After all, we both want the same thing, do we not?'

Emma smiled slightly. Should she tell him that it seemed to be Phyllida that Lord Hereward had been seeing, not Miss Stukeley? No, let him go on thinking it was the other.

Antony might yet prove useful. Besides, she was getting bored with Hereward's erratic appearances, and here was an attractive man bringing her roses. Emma felt that she deserved a little consolation, and perhaps Nell deserved to be taken down a peg or two for her ill-concealed relish in bringing her unwelcome news.

She inclined her head, smiled again and bade him sit down. 'Will you take a little wine and biscuits with me, Mr Herriot?'

'Thank you.'

Emma set herself out to charm, leaning against the arm of the *chaise-longue* with studied grace. 'Of course, little Miss Stukeley loves you to distraction,' she said, her large, dark eyes flicking him an admiring glance.

Antony saw it, leaned back in his chair and stretched his legs expansively. 'I believe so, but she's damned closely chaperoned.'

Obviously she would be, thought Emma. And the more closely she was chaperoned by her obnoxious cousin, the better pleased she, Emma, would be. 'I do not see how I could help,' she said, pouring him a glass of wine and handing it to him. 'A biscuit, Mr Herriot?'

'No thank you. I am simply asking that you keep Lord Hereward occupied, Miss Winter. As I am sure you can do.'

'You flatter me, sir.' Emma's breath quickened.

She might be losing her touch, thought

Antony, looking critically at her. She was a very beautiful woman, but men had been known to tire even of beautiful mistresses. 'I think not.' Antony put down his glass and came over to her. 'You are a very desirable woman, Emma. Lord Hereward would be mad to think of a skinny little thing like Araminta, when he has such loveliness to hand.' He reached out to stroke her slender neck where a pulse throbbed quickly.

Well, why not, thought Emma. Hereward was her bread and butter and she wanted him to marry her, but didn't a girl wish for a different jam every now and then? It was a long time since she had indulged herself. If Hereward could give her such a fright over some stupid widow, why shouldn't she take some man she fancied? Serve him right!

'Do you want to seal the bargain?' she asked Antony, her voice husky.

'You know I do.' Antony pressed his lips to where the pulse raced and allowed his hands to caress where his mouth would soon follow. He wondered whether the *chaise-longue* would be wide enough for both of them. And then he thought: she's mine in more ways than one. The enviable Emma will have to find some way of detaching Lord Hereward—if she doesn't want this little episode to get back to him.

*　　　*　　　*

154

In her drawing-room Mrs Osborne watched the four young people with satisfaction. It was all going very well; indeed, far from being backward, Lord Gifford was receiving the lion's share of the attention. Even Araminta was giggling at something he'd said, her eyes sparkling like emeralds.

Lord Hereward, silent for once, said very little, only watched the laughing group broodingly. Mrs Osborne sincerely hoped he was noting Araminta's youthful vivacity. Perhaps such unaccustomed seriousness was a hopeful sign? She would leave them together for a while, she decided. It may be that her presence was inhibiting. She had confidence enough in Phyllida to know that she would keep Araminta in line.

When she had gone the company rearranged themselves slightly, Thorold and Araminta sitting together on the window-seat and Phyllida and Hereward quietly overlooking them. Phyllida, acutely conscious of where Hereward was sitting, tried hard to absorb herself in the conversation with the others, but she did not know how often she was silent. Hereward, she knew, was looking at her, but he too was saying very little.

'I miss my Caroline,' Thorold was saying.

'Why do you not bring her to London then?' asked Araminta.

'Her nurse would never hear of it. She'd say it would upset her routine.'

'She can bring her routine with her,' said Araminta obstinately. Why shouldn't Caroline come if Lord Gifford wanted her to?

'And then Grandmama...' began Thorold.

'It's your house,' Araminta pointed out, 'Caroline's your daughter. You'd like to see her. I'm sure she'd like to see you. You have a garden and there are parks and the river.'

'There's a river at Maynard,' said Thorold gloomily.

'But the Thames is *different*; there are boats and wharves and things. Anyway, why shouldn't she come down if you want her to? She's your daughter, after all! Phyl and I would love to see her, wouldn't we, Phyl?'

Hereward, glancing at Phyllida, saw to his concern that she was wiping away a tear with her finger.

'Of course,' Phyllida smiled, her eyes too bright with unshed tears.

Hereward, so long inured to feminine tears, found himself unaccountably touched by this evidence of her distress and even more so by the unobtrusiveness with which she tried to hide it. Whatever it was he had stumbled on, she did not want it to become public property. He would respect that. Deftly he turned the conversation to Araminta's ball which was to take place in the middle of May, now barely ten days away.

'Then I shall be really grown-up,' said Araminta proudly.

156

'Do you think you will feel any different?' Thorold smiled tenderly at her.

'Why, yes!' said Araminta astonished.

Phyllida wrenched her mind away from her own thoughts and looked across at Thorold and Araminta, sitting cosily together on the window-seat and smiling at each other. What a well-suited couple they would make, she thought suddenly. Lord Gifford would give Araminta just that touch of fatherly protection she needed. It was plain too that the Earl found her cousin's vivacity to his taste. But perhaps it was just as well, she told herself sternly, that Mrs Osborne had set her sights elsewhere for Araminta. Lord Gifford was usually shy and retiring in company, she dreaded to think what Mrs Osborne's domineering tactics would do.

In this, Phyllida did her grandmother an injustice. Mrs Osborne was not so crude. Phyllida herself was not aware that she too was the subject of one of her grandmother's matrimonial plots.

Hereward caught Phyllida's wistful look at Thorold and Araminta and interpreted it differently. Perhaps his grandmother was right, he thought, perhaps Mrs Gainford did have an affection for his brother. He felt the anger rise up in him. Hereward was not much used to introspection and he did not know why he found the idea so distasteful. A Gainford to become Countess of Gifford, he told himself. Ridiculous! Why, she had not a penny to her name (he had quite forgotten his previous accusations of her ill-gotten gains) and her mother had eloped with an obscure gentleman of neither fortune nor importance. Phyllida was well-enough, he supposed. He acquitted her of being on the catch, but for her to hope to marry into the FitzIvors! It was quite absurd.

But somehow this reasoning did not satisfy him. It seemed, in some odd way, to miss out some vital connection, some necessary ingredient. Hereward tried to shrug off all thoughts of the previous evening. He wondered uncomfortably whether he had said too much about Johnny, whether Phyllida would presume on the intimacy and say something about it. She did not, and perversely, Hereward was then disappointed.

Suddenly Hereward could bear it no longer. He caught Thorold's eye and rose to go. When this visit was over he would forget all about Phyllida. He would go and spend the afternoon with Emma. Then he would feel differently. He would feel relaxed and content with his hedonistic bachelor existence. These stupid half-formed wishes to be drowned in those dark-green eyes, to touch that pale creamy skin, would vanish. He did not want to jettison his entire way of life, and for what? Intelligence and sympathy? He must be mad! No man in his senses would even consider giving up so satisfying and talented a mistress as Emma, merely because he wanted, unaccountably, to talk to some impecunious widow!

He did not talk to the impecunious widow and as a result spent the entire journey home wondering what she thought of his revelations about Johnny or whether she did indeed hope to marry his brother. He rigorously excluded any thoughts of wondering what she thought of the involuntary revelations about Emma. But all the same, he could not help seeing Phyllida's carefully expressionless face when he returned from the Knaresborough box and wishing that fate had not sent Emma to the opera that particular night.

*   *   *

Araminta's seventeen years had not taught her that it was necessary to do anything other than enjoy herself. Spoilt and indulged as she had been from her youth, it never crossed her mind to consider what effect her actions might have on anybody else. The evening at Vauxhall, however, had given her pause for thought.

For some days after the episode she revolved Antony's behaviour in her mind and contrasted it with Thorold's. She began, unwillingly, to see that her grandmother might be right in her restricted acceptance of him, and Phyllida not far off in hinting that he was a fortune-hunter. She had been a silly dupe, she thought, but she would not be so again.

Araminta, in the safety of her bed, allowed

her tears to flow and realized in the release of tension that she had indeed been in a very nasty position from which only her resourcefulness and the providential arrival of Lord Gifford had rescued her. She had gone with Antony trusting him to take care of her in what she had naïvely seen as a mere prank. He had betrayed that trust. If he'd really loved her, thought an older, wiser Araminta, he would not have abused her inexperience.

Accordingly, when Antony arrived the following day, complete with roses, Araminta greeted him with some reserve. She and Antony were more or less alone in the drawing-room, for Phyllida, who was there as chaperone, disliked Antony, and had merely given him her hand on arrival and retreated with her embroidery to the window-seat, leaving Antony and Araminta to sit on the sofa and talk undisturbed.

'I would never have hurt you, dearest,' whispered Antony. 'You know that.'

'I did not know,' retorted Araminta, 'and I preferred to take no chances.'

'That was a very naughty trick to play.' Antony tried to take her hand.

'Good!' Araminta removed it.

'I see you don't forgive me.' Antony put on his look of pathos.

'Of course I forgive you,' replied Araminta impatiently. 'Don't be silly, Antony. Let's forget it, shall we?'

Antony began to be angry. Araminta was looking at him with a certain calm friendliness, quite unlike her previous starry-eyed admiration, and he didn't like it. He was becoming quite hard-pressed for money; he did not want to waste more time in bringing the tiresome child back to a suitable state of adoration. But there was no help for it.

'I can't forget it! How can I be happy when I know that my foolish ardour has lost me the affection of the loveliest girl in the world?'

Araminta bit back the impatient retort that rose to her lips. She did not want to quarrel with him, besides he was Grandmama's godson and that might make things awkward. Anyway, she'd liked him well enough before, why shouldn't she again, once this silly business was over? Feeling virtuously grown-up, she decided that she would not hurt his feelings—she was too young to know that such charity would serve to make him feel ridiculous. And that, in so vain a man, could be dangerous.

'Phyl explained to me how foolish I was to go to Vauxhall and now I see that she was right.'

'You told your cousin?'

'Of course,' said Araminta mendaciously, for she had not. 'Are you worried that she will tell? I assure you you may be easy. She laughed when I told her and I promised not to do it again.'

She laughed! That dowdy, jumped-up, second-rate widow dared to laugh at his discomfiture? Antony darted Phyllida a look of pure malice. She thought she'd got the better of him, did she? Doubtless her grandmother was paying her well for this. Antony's eyes narrowed. He'd pay her out for her laughter, that and other interferences. He'd marry Araminta by hook or by crook and he'd take steps to see that Mrs Ambrose Gainford was well and truly disgraced.

*　　*　　*

Emma, meanwhile, was feeling very pleased with herself. Antony had proved to be a demanding lover, with a touch of brutal selfishness that she found very exciting. He had, in fact, left her with a number of bruises on her inner thigh that she was going to find very difficult to explain away. Still, by the time Hereward came they would probably have faded.

Then, she received a discreet note from the elder Mrs Gainford. *She knows*, it read, *and I think we have nothing more to worry about.* Emma folded it up and held it to the candle flame and watched, smiling, while Phyllida's hopes burnt to ashes.

All the same, she greeted Hereward's unexpected arrival that afternoon with a certain wariness. She had, in fact, glimpsed his carriage through the window, and sped upstairs. A headache and a shadowy bedroom would hide her bruises and explain any lapses.

'Where's Miss Winter?' enquired Hereward of Polly, as he strode into the house. 'In the drawing-room?'

'I think she's in the bedroom, my lord.'

'Good God! In the middle of the afternoon?' But he smiled at Polly, which made her feel all of a flutter as she later told the envious kitchen-maid, and handed her his cloak and hat. Polly watched him with a sigh as he went upstairs.

Emma sat at her dressing-table, an array of bottles in front of her. The lace curtains at the window filtered the light and gave the room a shadowy quality.

'Hereward!' Emma rose smiling.

'Whatever are you doing up here?'

'Oh, I had a slight headache, and then I thought I'd try some of this new pineapple water for the complexion.' She held up one scented cheek.

'Mm, very nice.' Hereward gave a short laugh. 'Well,' he said, 'you're always complaining that the *chaise-longue* is too slippery. We seem to be in a convenient place for once!' He tugged at his cravat impatiently and threw it on to a chair.

But somehow the resulting lovemaking was less than satisfactory. Emma behaved with her usual abandon. Hereward had duly lost himself awhile in the pleasures of her body, and

163

then what? All he felt as he lay, hands behind his head, gazing up at the canopy of the bed, was a corroding sense of disappointment. Nothing was wrong and yet something was missing. What the devil was the matter with him?

I needn't have bothered, thought Emma resentfully. He hadn't even noticed the bruises.

* * *

Antony sat in his room and stared at the empty grate. A renewed demand from his landlady had forced him to give her his few remaining guineas, and there, on the table in front of him, was a pile of letters. Doubtless mostly bills, for both his tailor and his shoemaker had become quite intrusively insistent recently. Damn it, a fellow had to dress properly, hadn't he? How the devil was he to gain admittance to those houses where the play was deepest if he wasn't correctly dressed?

What was more it was his birthday today, though he knew better than to expect more than a reproachful letter from his widowed mother living in reduced circumstances in Bath. Last year she had sent him a hand-knitted muffler! A muffler, when he needed money!

He flicked through the letters impatiently, then stopped. One had the Osborne crest on the envelope. Araminta? Puzzled, Antony opened it. Out fell a note from Mrs Osborne and a draft on her bank for £100. In the note she wished him a happy birthday, and remained his affectionate godmother, Cecilia Osborne.

Antony's first feeling was one of fury. He was being bought off! And for a derisory £100. Phyllida must have told Mrs Osborne, who was making it clear that he was to keep away from Araminta.

A moment's reflection would have told Antony that this was unlikely. Mrs Osborne had no reason to buy him off. If she had truly been told of the episode at Vauxhall, she could have forbidden him the house, or even ruined him socially; neither was beyond her powers. But cool rationality where his vanity was concerned had never been Antony's strong point.

He would have Araminta to wife whether his godmother liked it or not. The £100 was merely on account. What was needed was for Araminta to be compromised in such a way that it could not be hushed up: preferably by using her known impetuosity as the main contributory factor.

Antony didn't really care what happened to Araminta once they were married. If, somehow, the fault could be hers, then perhaps Mrs Osborne would receive them. If not, then Araminta could live with his mother in Bath. He would have no difficulty in returning to his former circles in Town, he knew that. A man with his racing tips and gambling expertise must always be acceptable.

He would have to carry Araminta off somewhere and stay overnight. Now what would appeal to her? A rescue mission, perhaps? But who or what? And how could he manage to drag Phyllida into it and cause her disgrace?

He would mull it over, he decided, while paying Emma a visit.

Emma greeted him with a peal of laughter. 'Splendid!' she cried. 'You look just like a music master!' For Antony was wearing a plain, dark suit and carried a small leather case.

Antony grimaced and threw the music case on to a chair.

'Darling, don't frown so! How else could you come here twice a week without Hereward knowing? Look, I've had the harp uncovered.'

Antony looked at it with dislike. 'Wherever did you get that thing? You don't play it surely?' He had spent enough unwilling hours listening to some daughter of the house on her harp. He did not want to hear it again.

'I bought it cheap from an old friend who once rented rooms to some French *émigrée* in Somers Town. *She'd* brought it to England during the Terror, I believe, and left it with my friend when she couldn't pay the rent.'

'You'd have thought she'd be too occupied escaping to have dragged her harp with her,'

166

said Antony, in tones of disgust.

'Well, she did. I bought it for a play I was in.' The play originally required Emma as Rosalba, Princess of Illyria, to be discovered by her lover playing the flute. Emma was having none of it, feeling that puffed-out cheeks would not enhance her reputation. She had acquired the harp instead, and learned to strum a few chords. What could be more natural than that she should wish to pick up her talents again and have a music master to teach her?

'But I don't play the damned thing,' Antony protested.

'It's not the *harp* I want you to play on,' responded Emma.

On this particular morning, their delightful duet over, Emma left Antony while she went upstairs to tidy herself. Antony dressed and then wandered round the room, picking up ornaments—hm, Sèvres—and looking at Emma's letters on her escritoire. Nothing much there. The escritoire had four little drawers. Two contained writing paper and envelopes. A third contained a seal with EW on it and some red sealing wax, a ball of string and some odds and ends. The fourth was locked.

Curious, thought Antony. There was no key. But he had not skirted the edges of respectability for nothing. His penknife contained a number of useful gadgets, among them a piece of stiff wire. Antony crossed the room and opened the door cautiously. Emma was still upstairs, he could hear her talking to her maid. He went back to the escritoire, took out the wire and in half a minute had opened the drawer. Inside were a couple of playbills with Emma's name on them, and a folded piece of paper tied with a ribbon, heavy, like parchment.

Swiftly, Antony took it out, undid the ribbon, opened it and whistled. Fate had just put the most perfect weapon into his hands.

There was the sound of footsteps coming down the stairs. Antony had just time to close the little drawer and stuff the paper into his music case before Emma came back into the room.

*   *   *

It was at Lady Albinia Marchmont's At Home one Thursday afternoon that Phyllida and Araminta first learnt that little Caroline FitzIvor had arrived in London with her nurse.

'I understand that Lord Gifford went up and collected her *himself*!' said Lady Albinia in tones of astonishment. She herself had not cared for children and had been only too glad to have them removed from her sight by nurses and nurserymaids: the thought of anybody, particularly a *man*, voluntarily wishing to see his daughter seemed to her incredible.

'It is certainly very odd,' echoed Mrs

Osborne disapprovingly. 'Lord Gifford has been reading too much Rousseau, a very underbred man in my opinion. Children should be kept in the nursery. Change is so very unsettling.'

'Don't know that I'd care to have any brat of mine hanging round all the time,' Barnabas Marchmont laughed, his pendulous cheeks wobbling. 'Children should be seen and not heard, that's what I always say!'

'Just imagine what Mr Marchmont's child would look like, Phyl,' whispered Araminta. 'A fat little piglet!'

'I think it's so romantic, don't you, Mrs Gainford?' cried Miss Lucy Telford, artlessly.

'Why romantic?' asked Phyllida.

'Oh, well, the lonely widower, you know, sunk in melancholy. What can cheer his anguished heart but his infant daughter's innocent prattle!'

'But he's not a bit like that!' cried Araminta.

Lucy looked affronted and Phyllida said soothingly, 'It is true that Lord Gifford is a quiet man, but I don't think he's quite so grief-stricken as you imagine, Miss Lucy. Time heals most wounds, you know.'

Lucy blushed and stammered something, for she was somewhat in awe of Phyllida and had just remembered that she, too, had been widowed.

'I do hope we shall see little Caroline soon,' said Araminta eagerly in the carriage going home.

Her wish was to be gratified. The next day brought a note from Lady Gifford asking if the girls might come to tea that afternoon. Thorold was very anxious that they should meet his daughter. She did hope that they would not mind having tea up in the nursery, but the nurse was anxious that Caroline's routine should be interrupted as little as possible.

From which Phyllida gathered that Lady Gifford too had disapproved of Thorold's impetuous move. The girls accepted.

As soon as luncheon was finished Araminta rushed upstairs and began to throw dresses and shawls all over her bed. She knocked impatiently on Phyllida's bedroom door.

'Do come through, Phyl. Whatever am I going to wear? What do you think of my new hyacinth silk? Or the floral print with the little ruff? Will Lord ... I mean Lady Gifford like it, do you think?'

'I think Lord, or even Lady Gifford will think you look delightful in whatever you choose to wear,' said Phyllida teasingly.

'And my hair,' Araminta rushed on, betraying only by the faintest flush that she had heard Phyllida's comments. 'Should I get Hetty to frizz it at the front, perhaps?'

'I think you look very pretty as you are,' replied Phyllida calmly. Araminta's red curls were caught up in a light knot at the back of her head and loose ringlets allowed to fall down.

'But it's so *boring*,' said Araminta impatiently. 'I've had it this way for ever.'

Phyllida laughed, 'Only since I arrived. Before that I'm sure that you had a neat schoolgirl's braid.'

'Plaits!' said Araminta shuddering.

'I should wear something simple, if I were you,' said Phyllida as she went back to her room. 'Sticky little fingers will not improve your new silk, you know.'

When Phyllida came downstairs later to greet an impatient Araminta in the hall, she was not entirely surprised to see that her cousin had chosen to wear her hyacinth-blue silk, deeply flounced and decorated with knots of deep blue ribbon. Phyllida herself wore a simple cambric dress, embroidered with lilies-of-the-valley, and pale-green slippers on her feet. She carried a small parcel, together with her reticule in one hand.

'It's only a little toy dog you pull along on wheels,' she explained as Araminta looked enquiringly at it. 'I nipped out and bought it in Grafton Street this morning. Would you like to give it to Caroline with me?'

Araminta kissed her. 'You *are* kind, Phyl.'

'Very well then, let's go.'

Lady Caroline FitzIvor, a dark-haired moppet with wide brown eyes, hid behind her nurse's skirts at the sight of four giants entering her nursery. The yellow trousers she knew

171

belonged to her papa, and the grey ones to her Uncle Hereward, and when the company sat down and became a more reasonable height, Caroline peeked out and saw that it was indeed her papa and with him were two beautiful ladies.

She allowed her nurse to put her into her high-chair and stared at Araminta, whose hair fascinated her.

'Pitty,' she remarked.

'Yes, isn't she,' responded Thorold, delighted with this evidence of his daughter's high level of intelligence.

'Isn't she lovely, Phyl!' exclaimed Araminta.

'Yes indeed,' said Phyllida quietly.

Hereward looked at her from his vantage point beyond the tea trolley. Her face was white and strained and she was looking at Caroline with a sort of anguish. Hereward glanced at the others, but nobody had noticed, being too occupied with crowing over Caroline's squeaks and gurgles. He looked back at Phyllida and the expression that so disturbed him had vanished. She was eating her piece of seed cake and smiling as Caroline held out a sticky finger of bread and jam to her father.

'Thank you, darling,' said Thorold heroically.

'You are a very good father, Lord Gifford.' Araminta looked at him with shining eyes. She could not remember her own father doing

172

more than giving her an absent-minded pat and a 'run away now'.

Thorold smiled at her. 'My one unqualified success,' he replied. 'I know I'm an awkward sort of chap in other situations but...'

'I know that is not true,' said Araminta in a low voice.

There was a pause.

'Perhaps,' said Thorold hesitantly, 'in time, you might....'

But whatever he had been going to say was halted by a shriek from Nurse as Caroline, resenting the attention being removed from herself, banged her tray hard with her cup and milk flew everywhere.

After tea, Phyllida handed Araminta the parcel. Araminta offered it to Caroline who pounced on it, sat down on the carpet, her fat little legs sticking out in front of her, and tugged at the paper impatiently.

'Dog! Dog!' she cried.

'What an excellent choice, Miss Stukeley,' said Thorold. 'Not too big for her.'

'It was Phyllida's choice,' said Araminta reluctantly, 'but it's from both of us.'

'If you don't mind, Lord Gifford,' interrupted the nurse firmly, 'I should like to get Lady Caroline tidied up now. If you would like to go to the drawing-room I'll bring her down to you presently.'

'Or we could go outside,' put in Hereward. 'It's a pity to be indoors on such a lovely day.'

Thorold glanced out of the window. 'It's quite dry,' he said. 'What do you think, Nurse? Could Caroline come outside for a while?'

'Certainly, my lord. I'll change her into her boots and coat. It'll do her good to be in the garden after that nasty cramped carriage.'

Hereward glanced at Phyllida and smiled. 'A Parthian shot,' he said in a low voice. 'I didn't think Thorold would get away with his high-handed action in bringing Caroline to London that easily.'

'Lady Caroline's spirits do not seem to have suffered from the journey,' replied Phyllida, smiling back.

The garden behind the Gifford house in St James's Square was surprisingly large. There was a formal garden by the house with little box hedges, gravel footpaths and some cone-shaped conifers. Behind that was a lawn, neatly edged with flower beds. Then there was a rose trellis with an archway leading to a small shrubbery.

'But this is charming,' cried Phyllida, as she took Hereward's arm and descended the stone steps into the formal garden.

'It's very old-fashioned, I'm afraid, all these geometric shapes. But Grandmama likes it so.'

'It's very restful. Mm, camomile.'

'I see you're a connoisseur.'

'I'm very fond of my garden at home where I have a herb bed. Mostly for cooking, but also for remedies for the village people. I grow camomile for a sluggish liver.'

'Good heavens! And are you successful?'

'Often enough. These old remedies are usually well-tried, you know.'

'You become more interesting every day, Mrs Gainford,' said Hereward. Phyllida felt the colour rise to her cheeks at the warmth in his voice, but could find no light rejoinder. They had now crossed the lawn and were by the rose arbour at the edge of the shrubbery. They turned to look back at the house, its walls golden in the afternoon sun. 'Ah, here comes Caroline and her nurse. Would you like to go back?'

Phyllida watched as Thorold and Araminta turned to greet the arrivals, Caroline toddling towards Thorold, her little arms outstretched. 'Up! Up!' she cried. Thorold picked her up.

Phyllida turned away.

'Are you all right, Mrs Gainford?'

Phyllida shook her head as if imploring his silence. Hereward could see the trace of a tear coursing down her half-hidden cheek, and her ragged breathing.

'Here!' he said. 'take my arm. We'll go into the shrubbery. We shan't be disturbed there.'

Blindly Phyllida allowed him to lead her under the rose arch and into the shrubbery. There in the centre, surrounded by laurels and holly, was a small statue of Pan, sitting on a rock and playing his pipes. By it was a wrought-iron bench and it was to those that

175

Hereward guided her.

Phyllida sank down, covered her face with her hands and burst into tears. She cried unrestrainedly for several minutes as if with a sorrow too great to be borne in silence any longer. Hereward watched her with concern, but said nothing.

At last Phyllida gave a great sigh and sat up, groping for her reticule. Hereward handed it to her. She took out her handkerchief, blew her nose firmly, brushed at her eyes and stood up shakily.

Hereward pulled her down again. 'Sit down. Your face is all blotchy and your nose is red. They'll fade if we give them five minutes or so.' He added after a moment, 'Don't be afraid, I shan't ask any questions, and nobody shall hear of this from me.'

They sat in silence for a minute or so, then Phyllida said quietly, 'You see, she's almost the same age as Rosina would have been.'

'Rosina?'

'Ambrosine. My daughter. She died of diphtheria when she was just eight months old.'

Hereward took Phyllida's hand in a comforting clasp. 'Tell me about her,' he commanded.

'She was born in February last year and died in November. I only had her for such a short while!' Phyllida turned her head away again.

'And you miss her very much.'

176

'Yes! Yes!' wept Phyllida.

'Does Mrs Osborne know about her?'

'No! Only Mrs Gainford. I wrote to her again after I had her letter repudiating me, to tell her of Rosina's birth, but I had no reply.'

Hereward frowned in an effort to disentangle this. 'What's this? Mrs Gainford refused to acknowledge you? But I saw her speaking to you at the opera.' He let go of her hand.

Phyllida blew her nose again. 'I wrote to Mrs Gainford after Ambrose was killed, telling her that we were married, which I think Ambrose had put off doing,' she explained more clearly. 'I also told her that I was expecting his child. She wrote me *such* a letter. Even now I cannot bear to think about it.'

'But what on earth did she say? I would have thought she'd be positively delighted that Gainford had settled down respectably at last and that there was a grandchild on the way.'

'Yes, now I wonder at it myself. But then, I was still so raw. What with the terrible battle, even now I dream of those piles of broken bodies, the mud, the blood...' She shook her head. 'And then it was several days before they found Ambrose's body. Then the burial and the difficulties of selling some of his things to get home. I just couldn't think straight. I accepted that she didn't want to know me and put it out of my mind.'

'But the baby!'

'Yes, that's why I wrote after Rosina was born. By that time the first grief was over, and she was so perfect. I suppose I thought Mrs Gainford might have changed her mind.'

'Do you mean that you have never had a penny from her?'

'No.'

'Disgraceful! The Gainfords are not wealthy, and he's a miser, but to refuse to support a daughter-in-law!' He paused and then added, 'I can see now that my remarks when I first met you on the subject of your mother-in-law must have hurt you deeply, and I am sorry for them.'

Phyllida smiled. 'That is long past, my lord. It was Mrs Gainford who extended the olive branch and invited me to tea. I went, feeling that no good could be achieved by rancour.'

'You are far more forgiving than she deserves,' said Hereward warmly.

Phyllida shook her head. 'I am not at all forgiving. I dislike her intensely. She made me feel as if I was somehow at fault and that she and my grandmother had magnanimously decided to overlook it! I was very angry, I can tell you.'

'So why was she so eager to renew the acquaintance at the opera?'

Phyllida looked down at her hands for a moment before replying, 'I believe she felt obliged to bring me up to date on various pieces of social gossip.'

178

Hereward stared inscrutably into the laurels. 'I see,' he said dryly at last.

*   *   *

Antony, his sartorial elegance now enhanced by the fob watch he had been able to redeem from pawn, sat in his rooms, frowning deeply at the carpet. At last his brow cleared. He opened the parchment he had taken from Emma and smiled. It was not a pleasant smile, certainly not for the recipient of the little surprise he was planning.

He rang the bell for his man-servant. 'I'm just going out, Timms,' he said, 'I don't know when I may be back.'

'Very good, sir. And if anybody calls?'

'Tell them I am gone to pay a call on Lady Selina Lemmon!'

CHAPTER SEVEN

Emma Winter looked at the letter in front of her and sighed, half impatiently. It was from her old friend, Dick Burge, now Assistant Manager at the new Coburg Theatre.

You must come and see us, wrote Dick in his chatty way. *At the moment I'm working in a little hut on the site with builders and dust*

179

everywhere! But it's going to be quite splendid when it's finished, especially with Prince Leopold and Princess Charlotte taking an interest. This is going to be the place to be.

Emma stared unseeing out of the window: all at once the smell of greasepaint and the flare of the new gas-lights came flooding back. Ale and oysters at midnight after a show, the camaraderie in the green room, her old dresser, Abby, with her fund of salacious stories ... she shook herself firmly. There was also the gruelling hours, the flea-bitten lodgings, the numbed fingers in the dressing-room in winter, she must not forget those.

All the same, she turned back to Dick's letter eagerly.

We are planning to open in May next year, it continued. *A mixed bill, I think. A melodramatic spectacle, 'Trial by Battle', I'm sure you know the kind of thing, one of those with a cast of thousands. Then a Grand Asiatic Ballet called 'Alzora and Nerine' and the usual-type Harlequinade, 'Midnight Revelry'.*

The thing is, Emma my love, would you consider the part of Nerine? I'm not yet sure what we could offer you, but the money will be good—especially for you. What I need is the go-ahead to put it to the committee and then we can negotiate an offer.

I know that this is a long time in advance—we shan't start rehearsing until March '18, but if I could persuade you, then of course, your name would feature very prominently on all the advance billing. Anyway, think about it Emma. I don't really need to know until after the summer—just floating the idea.
Yours ever,
Dick

Emma allowed herself to dwell on the possibility that she might have both Hereward *and* the part of Nerine, but reluctantly dismissed it. Hereward would never consent. In any case, if she hoped to persuade him to make her Lady Hereward, then she would have to lead a life of the utmost decorum and (relative) chastity.

All the same she picked up the letter and went to put it in her escritoire. The private drawer slid open easily. Odd, thought Emma momentarily, I'm sure I locked it. She pushed Dick's letter on top of the playbills, locked it with the tiny key she wore round her neck and forgot about it.

*　　*　　*

Plans for Araminta's ball were now proceeding apace. The dustsheets were removed from the chandeliers in the ballroom and every crystal

181

taken down and washed by excited housemaids. Delivery boys began to stagger in with hampers under the watchful eye of the housekeeper. Flowers were ordered to decorate the ballroom and jardinières unearthed from the conservatory and stood newly cleaned against the walls.

Phyllida asked if she might help but was waved away impatiently by Mrs Osborne who liked to have everything under her own thumb, which meant, in effect, that the entire staff were on the point of mutiny. Already the under parlour-maid had had hysterics and Phyllida soon found that her unofficial role was to soothe the ruffled sensibilities in the basement and listen to the housekeeper's long-winded complaints.

'I never have any trouble with my servants,' Phyllida heard her grandmother say during a morning call. 'I believe in being very firm: it is the only way in my opinion.'

Phyllida smiled grimly, well aware that it was only her ministrations which had prevented two of the maids from giving notice. The cook too, amid a flurry of gestures indicative of his despair and a storm of French, of which Phyllida fortunately understood very little, threatened to leave. Mrs Osborne had presented him with a receipt of her own for the *filets de volaille à la maréchale* which he would find unquestionably superior. Maître Gautier rapidly reached boiling point. It had taken

Phyllida half the afternoon to soothe him—it was quite impossible, she assured him, that anybody's receipt could be superior to his. She respectfully suggested that he took no notice; a man of his intelligence must surely know that it was only Mrs Osborne's way.

To Phyllida's great pleasure Major and Mrs Quentin were attending the ball. Mrs Osborne had been favourably impressed by the Major on the occasion of his paying a call, and agreed to send them a card. If it crossed her mind that the friendship of so obviously respectable a couple (she had looked up Mrs Quentin in *Country Families of the United Kingdom* and was she not a Martindale?) would benefit her granddaughter's social standing by conferring some acceptability on her unfortunate marriage, she was tactful enough not to mention it. She would take care to introduce the Quentins to Lady Gifford, she thought.

She also sent Phyllida to pay a call on her mother-in-law. Phyllida went most reluctantly: the idea that Mrs Gainford's presence was needed at the ball to secure her, Phyllida's, position, revolted her.

In her matrimonial machinations, Mrs Osborne had not forgotten her plans for Araminta. She recognized two things: one was that at seventeen Araminta was perhaps a little young to be considering marriage and the other was that Lord Hereward was a far harder nut to crack. It was possible that Lord Gifford

183

might be persuaded into offering for Phyllida by the combined efforts of his grandmother and herself. It was extremely unlikely that Lord Hereward would be so complaisant. Phyllida and Lord Gifford must be married first, she decided. Then what could be more natural than that her cousin visited her? Hereward was already taken with Araminta, she could see from his frequent visits, that liking would be sure to deepen during a long summer at Maynard in Araminta's company.

She would take the opportunity of Phyllida's absence to take Araminta some way into her confidence.

Araminta was summoned to her boudoir.

'Of course, Lord Gifford will open the ball with you,' pronounced her ladyship. 'That is as it should be. But after that I want to make sure that he is given every opportunity to dance with Phyllida.'

'With Phyllida?' echoed Araminta.

'Certainly,' responded Mrs Osborne calmly. 'Lady Gifford and I have every expectation of them making a match of it.'

Araminta stood stock still from shock, her little face drained of all colour. Suddenly, she was acquainted with her own heart. She raised her hands slowly to her breast to still its beating and said in an odd voice, 'Does Ph ... Phyllida agree to this?'

'Good heavens, miss, I don't know,' said Mrs Osborne impatiently. 'She is a sensible girl, and after so disastrous a first marriage, I hope that she will do as she is told. Now don't bother me, Araminta. All you have to do is to be polite to Lord Gifford and find something agreeable to say about your cousin. That is not too difficult, surely?'

'No, Grandmama,' said Araminta in a colourless voice and left the room.

When Phyllida returned from paying her call on Mrs Gainford, she found Araminta up in the morning-room staring listlessly out of the window.

'Abominable woman,' cried Phyllida as she entered. 'Such insinuating manners! I'm not surprised Ambrose left home as he did. Why— whatever is the matter, love?'

For Araminta had broken down and was sobbing unrestrainedly into the cushions. Phyllida crossed to her at once, knelt down beside the sobbing girl and put an arm around her.

'What is it?' she coaxed. 'Grandmama again?' Araminta only cried louder. 'You know she doesn't mean all she says.'

Araminta raised her tear-stained face and cried desperately, 'You don't want to marry Lord Gifford, do you Phyl?'

'Marry Lord Gifford!' echoed Phyllida in astonishment. 'Whatever gave you that idea?'

'Grandmama did. And *I* want to, most dreadfully.'

*   *   *

Mrs Osborne was determined that Araminta's ball be the high point of the season. No expense was to be spared. The buffet supper (with or without the *filets de volaille à la maréchale*) was to be lavish, the champagne to flow in unlimited quantities. In the card-room unbroken packs of cards sat on every table. Extra lights had been placed outside in the street and a carpet spread out over the pavement, so that ladies' slippers might not become dusty as they descended from their carriages and walked to the house.

Araminta, after her talk with Phyllida, and hearing her cousin's own suspicions as to Lord Gifford's interest, was looking positively radiant. She stood with Mrs Osborne and Phyllida at the head of the stairs to receive the guests, her elfin beauty making most of the other girls look somehow ordinary. Her hair was shining with a coppery glow and was caught up by Hetty's clever fingers into loops and curls on top of her head, threaded in and out with tiny seed pearls. Her dress was of white silk, embellished with little pale-green silk knots.

When Thorold came up the stairs with Lady Gifford and Hereward, he just looked. Araminta cast Phyllida a mischievous glance and gave him her hand. Thorold took it as though it was a rare and precious flower.

186

'Miss ... Miss Stukeley,' he stammered, 'may I have the honour of the first two dances with you?'

'Yes,' said Araminta sunnily.

Thorold was still holding her hand and it wasn't until Lady Gifford cleared her throat that he belatedly released it, recollected himself and dutifully asked Phyllida for the next two dances.

Phyllida, standing quietly beside Araminta, looked covertly at Lord Hereward and her heart sank. She hadn't seen him since that day in the garden. Whatever must he think of her now? She was sure that she could trust him not to repeat anything, but the recollection of how she had betrayed her deepest emotions left her feeling acutely vulnerable.

Hereward was looking quite impossibly handsome. His golden hair, combed into windswept curls *à la Titus*, and his blue eyes were set off by his corbeau-coloured evening coat, embroidered waistcoat and black florentine silk breeches. He would never need to wear a corset such as she was sure Mr Barnabas Marchmont was, thought Phyllida, glancing at that portly young man coming up behind the Gifford party.

However, when she dared to glance up at Hereward, he was smiling down at her with such warmth in his eyes that her heart turned over. She put out her hand automatically and hoped that whatever she said was proper, for she had not the faintest idea what it was.

'I don't believe that we have danced together before, Mrs Gainford,' Hereward was saying. 'May I have the pleasure of the first two dances with you?'

'I should be honoured, my lord.'

Then Hereward was swept on by the crowd coming up the stairs and Phyllida reluctantly turned her attention to Lady Albinia Marchmont.

*   *   *

Antony greeted Araminta with a teasing friendliness which did much to dispel her wariness of him. He gave her no significant looks or squeezes of the hand, instead he reminded her how he used to call her carrot tops and added that now she was such a beautiful young lady he wouldn't dare.

'You used to pull my pig-tails as well!' Araminta reminded him.

'I hope you tipped the ink-pot over me for such an outrage!' replied Antony, laughing. 'Will you forgive me and allow me to have at least one country dance?'

'Of course. The first two after supper?'

Mrs Osborne smiled at this badinage. Antony had written her a very pretty letter thanking her for his birthday present and she was pleased with him. He was not putting himself forward in any way, indeed, he seemed much improved. She would write to his mother and say so. Poor Mary had had so much trouble with him. She would make it her pleasant duty to apprise her of the change in her son.

Antony bowed to Phyllida and complimented her on her looks, but Phyllida felt uneasy. There was something about his smile, a sort of gloating, that made her feel as if the emotions lurking underneath that well-mannered exterior were very different. She was pleased that the two dances he asked for were taken: sometimes it was a relief to be engaged to dance even with Mr Marchmont!

Antony said he was sorry, bowed again, and left her. Phyllida, still feeling uneasy, watched him go up the stairs. Then he half-turned and she saw him bow and nod very slightly to Lady Selina Lemmon, almost as if it was some prearranged signal. But that was ridiculous. Phyllida mentally took herself in hand and turned to greet the next guest.

All the same, she could not rid herself of the idea that there was some sort of league between Lady Selina and Antony Herriot, though what it could possibly be she had no idea.

*　　*　　*

Araminta and Thorold opened the ball with fitting grace and gravity. Thorold, who was not used to dancing, was concentrating on his steps and Araminta was feeling cautiously hopeful, coupled with an acute sense of her own inadequacy with regard to Thorold. He was older than she was, so much more intelligent and thoughtful, surely he must find her silly and schoolgirlish? And then his rescuing her at Vauxhall! Whatever must he think of her modesty in consenting to such a mad exploit? How could she convince him, if indeed he wanted to know, that she truly loved him, as she now realized she did?

Her unusual introspection made her silent. When the dance ended they had not exchanged more than half-a-dozen words.

'I'm sorry to be so dull,' muttered Thorold. 'I'm not sure of the steps, you see. It's been so long ... I don't want to let you down.'

'Oh no! No!'

'Never mind, I'm sure you'll find far livelier partners before the evening's over.'

'But I don't want any other partner!' cried Araminta desperately and then stopped.

'You don't?' asked Thorold slowly. Araminta shook her head, her face averted. All he could see was one pink cheek.

'You ... I ... oh, it's impossible!'

The music started again. Frowning and grim, Thorold took her hand to lead her into the set. Araminta held her head high and tried not to allow her lips to tremble. But she could not prevent her voice from shaking slightly as she answered some commonplace remark at

190

random. The dance continued through its paces. Thorold took Araminta's other hand and took the required step towards her before allowing her to turn under his arm. She looked strained and unhappy and suddenly he could bear it no longer, no matter how she might laugh at him.

'Araminta,' he whispered as the steps drew them momentarily closer.

Araminta looked up, hope in her eyes.

'May I come and talk to you? Alone. Tomorrow? About eleven?'

*   *   *

Miss Lucy Telford, who had unfortunately arrived too late to secure a partner for the first dance, sat with her sister on the gilt chairs around the edge of the ballroom. Both sisters were dressed in pink, with similar wreaths of pink rosebuds in their hair.

'Isn't she lovely, Mrs Gainford, I mean,' whispered Lucy, watching Phyllida dance with Lord Hereward. 'They are both such graceful dancers. I wish I were as confident as that!'

'You admire Mrs Gainford?' enquired Lady Selina, who happened to be sitting next to Lucy.

'Oh, so much!'

'I wonder if you'll admire her quite so much by the end of the evening,' said Lady Selina cryptically.

'Whatever did she mean?' whispered Lucy to her sister, when Lady Selina had gone.

Margaret shrugged, she was rather tired of hearing of Phyllida's perfections. 'I don't know.'

'Probably jealous, the old cat,' said Lucy.

Phyllida herself was feeling all the discomforts of being in love with few of its pleasures. Her relationship with Hereward was compounded of such disparate elements, fear, intimacy and suspicion, that now she was not at all sure of how he regarded her, if indeed he thought of her at all. It was impossible to be intimate at a ball and yet dancing with him, holding his hand for the various steps, passing under his arm, everything about being his partner gave her the most agonizing sense of physical closeness.

She could not help remembering how it had been with Ambrose. She always knew that when he came in of an evening and put an arm around her waist or reached for her hand, it would end in breathless and exhilarating lovemaking on the creaking wooden bedstead in their cheap and shabby lodgings. She blushed at her thoughts, but could not dismiss them.

She truly believed that she loved Hereward, that the intimacy of their conversations was precious to her, but she also desired him. And he was very happy with Miss Emma Winter.

That was the trouble with being a widow,

thought Phyllida. Young, unmarried girls did not have these shocking thoughts—at least, they had never occurred to her in her maiden days. And yet, would she really want just to be Hereward's mistress? Had she not learned slowly and painfully since Ambrose's death, that allowing herself to be vulnerable to other people, to be close, in short to love, was just as necessary to her? The thought struck her, unwillingly, that perhaps she had never loved Ambrose. She had desired him, but that was not the same thing. She could not think of a single occasion when they had ever discussed their own hopes and fears as she had with Hereward.

It was precisely *because* she understood more of Hereward's complexities that she could not deal in coquettish or come-hither glances. She wanted him to stay, so he had to be free to go. It was as simple as that.

When her two dances with Hereward ended, Phyllida could only be relieved.

Antony, standing quietly by a pillar, overheard various compliments to his godmother on the brilliance of the ball and the beauty of her granddaughters.

'So charming, so unaffected, both of them,' said Lady Vavasour. 'I declare this will be the most talked-of ball of the Season!'

You are right, it will be, thought Antony. Only not quite in the way you may imagine.

'Isn't this wonderful, Phyl?' cried Araminta

breathlessly as they passed each other during a dance. Her eyes were shining like stars.

'Yes, indeed.'

'I wish it might go on for ever!'

Phyllida was being taken in to supper by Major Quentin. 'I know you ought to have some young gallant to squire you,' said the Major, 'but Hester and I both want to talk to you, and there seems no other opportunity.'

'I shall be delighted to see both you and Mrs Quentin,' said Phyllida sincerely.

Phyllida had just left Mr Marchmont and moved thankfully towards Major and Mrs Quentin and the supper break, when Fate struck. In the pause between the last notes of the orchestra and the succeeding hubbub of voices, Lady Selina's voice came over clearly.

'Of course, I've always said it, that red-headed madam's a fraud!'

'To whom are you referring, Lady Selina?' enquired Mrs Osborne, raising her eyebrows and wondering what on earth had made her put up with Lady Selina and her ill manners all these years.

'Your granddaughter, Mrs Osborne, the so-called Mrs Ambrose Gainford.'

There was a gasp from the assembled guests—either of horror or pleasure according to their several dispositions. But everybody wanted to hear more.

'Perhaps it's time you retired quietly, Mrs Osborne,' continued Lady Selina with

194

venomous relish. 'Society does not care to have impostors foisted on them.'

Hereward pushed his way to the front, his face set with suspicion. 'I assume you have grounds for this extraordinary accusation,' he asked. 'If Mrs Gainford is *not* Mrs Gainford, then who, pray, is she?'

'She is, as she always was, Miss Danby,' spat out Lady Selina.

'Come, Lady Selina,' said Sir Marmaduke firmly, in a voice that had quelled any number of subordinates in his time, 'Mrs Ambrose Gainford is here, her mother-in-law is here, let us hear what they have to say.'

Several hundred pairs of eyes turned towards Phyllida, who was standing white-faced and frozen with shock. Mrs Quentin took her hand in a comforting clasp. Phyllida opened her mouth, but could say nothing. Everything had the air of a nightmare about it. Surely she would wake up and find it had all been a horrible dream. But people were looking at her, eyes both curious and hostile boring into her. Her eyes filled with tears.

Mrs Quentin squeezed her hand reassuringly and said in a calm voice, 'Mrs Ambrose Gainford was married by our regimental chaplain. I was there myself. And, in the absence of her father, Major Quentin gave her away.'

At this moment Mrs Gainford, who had been watching the scene from the shelter of

Miss Heywood's arm now broke into hysterical tears.

'I knew she'd return to plague us!' she cried. 'It's all *your* fault.' She turned angrily to Phyllida. 'If you'd stayed quietly in the country as you were meant to do, this would never have happened.'

'But ... but I don't understand,' whispered Phyllida, bewildered. 'Why should I have stayed in the country?'

Araminta let go of Thorold's hand which had somehow become joined to hers, ran to Phyllida and put her arms around her. 'It is quite impossible that Phyl has done anything wrong!' she cried.

'Very affecting,' sneered Lady Selina, 'but we must remember that your own position in Society is caught up in Miss Danby's little charade.'

'Lady Selina, you have not answered Mrs Quentin,' said Sir Marmaduke sternly. 'If she and her husband were at the wedding, then there must have been a marriage. Unless you are giving them the lie?'

'Possibly Miss Danby went through a form of marriage and doubtless Major and Mrs Quentin were duped like the rest of us. Augusta Gainford does not seem so certain of her ground as you are, Sir Marmaduke!'

Mrs Gainford was uttering such shuddering moans that several people now came forward and assisted her and Miss Heywood to some chairs and offered sal volatile.

'Let her have spasms,' declared Lady Selina. 'I daresay she'd rather have 'em than tell us what's been going on.'

Major Quentin, who had taken an acute dislike to Lady Selina said, 'I can testify that Mrs Ambrose Gainford was married. I gather you are saying that the marriage was not legal, Lady Selina. Perhaps you would care to prove it?'

'Certainly.' Lady Selina directed a quick glance of triumph at Antony, standing silent at the side of the room, watching the scene with a quiet enjoyment, his eyes moving round to see how the main protagonists were taking each move. She opened her reticule, took out a piece of crackling paper and unfolded it. 'Here it is. The marriage was not valid because Captain Ambrose Richard Charles Gainford was already married!'

A wail rose from Mrs Gainford. Lady Selina ignored it. 'Consequently the oh-so-correct Mrs Ambrose Gainford does not exist—here. The person—for lady I cannot call her—who has been foisted on us was his mistress!'

It was a lie, it was all false, thought Phyllida over and over again. We were never really married, and he knew it. It was a deliberate lie.

Hereward had been staring first at Phyllida's shocked face and then at Mrs Gainford's contorted one. 'I begin to see now,' he said, addressing Mrs Gainford in tones of ice. 'I

197

wondered why you had not acknowledged Mrs Ambrose Gainford after her husband's death—nor allowed her even a widow's portion.'

'Very true,' put in Mrs Quentin. 'The poor love had to sell her husband's watch to buy her passage home. She wrote to me that her mother-in-law said she disapproved of the marriage and would give her nothing.'

'I knew nothing of it!' cried Mrs Gainford desperately. 'Nothing!'

'The truth is,' went on Hereward scornfully, 'that you knew very well that the marriage was invalid. I have no doubt that it was one of those injudicious early entanglements and that you bought the woman off. I daresay that you hoped that by repudiating Mrs Ambrose and knowing that she would be short of money, possibly of even the barest necessities, you hoped to silence her forever. You are despicable!'

'How was I to know that Mrs Osborne would take her up again?' wailed Mrs Gainford.

'I *told* you not to meddle,' said Miss Heywood suddenly to Phyllida. 'I *said* you'd repent it. And now you see?'

'It's not *Phyl's* fault if everybody has been lying to her,' cried Araminta indignantly.

'How do we know that Miss Danby wasn't lying as well?' returned Lady Selina silkily.

Lady Gifford stepped forward, one hand

firmly grasping her ebony cane. 'This has gone on long enough,' she said. 'What Miss Heywood said just now must absolve Mrs Ambrose Gainford from any collusion: her respectability is beyond question. What I *do* question, Lady Selina, is *your* motive in offering this information in so very public a place. Are you quite certain that you have no axe of your own to grind?'

'Hear, hear,' muttered Major Quentin.

Lady Selina's sharp face looked quite pinched with spite. Ever since Princess Caroline's ignominious retreat her position had declined from the important and sought-after to being a mere hanger-on, dependent on the good will of others—especially such condescension as Lady Gifford's. It was not to be borne. Even as a schoolgirl Lady Selina had found it hard to accept without rancour the grudging acceptability that her difficult personality had brought her and time had not changed her. So it was with a malicious pleasure that she prepared her trump card.

'My motives are only to expose the impostors. It may interest you to know, Lady Gifford, that it touches your august family too! Though, naturally, I wouldn't *dream* of suggesting that *you* were engaged in any covering up.' Her tone of voice said otherwise.

She paused for effect and allowed her gaze to travel slowly round the room. 'Only your grandson had the sense not to offer to marry the creature.'

Thorold moved to Lady Gifford's side and stood beside her. Good heavens, thought Lady Gifford incongruously, surely *Drusilla* hadn't married Captain Gainford as well!

'Captain Gainford, you see, was first married to Miss Emma Winter!'

In a few angry strides Hereward had crossed the room and seized the paper that Lady Selina was gleefully waving.

'Emma Winter,' said Major Quentin musingly, 'yes, that was the girl's name.'

'What's that?' demanded Hereward, turning to him.

'It was during the summer of '14. Gainford was in Brighton. The woman he had in keeping, an actress I think she was, was Emma Winter. She must have cost him a pretty penny, I can tell you. Beautiful, as I remember, but quite insatiable.'

'She hasn't changed,' said Hereward grimly. He folded the licence and put it in his pocket.

'Excuse me, Lord Hereward,' said Lady Selina. 'That is mine.'

'I beg your pardon, ma'am. The marriage lines traditionally belong to the lady. I shall restore them to their rightful owner. Personally.'

He glanced round the assembled company, his eyes resting for one brief expressionless moment on Phyllida, and walked out.

It was the signal for the ball to break up.

200

Antony remained standing by the wall and laughed silently. Lady Selina had surpassed herself, he thought. He must congratulate her on her performance sometime. But not now. What was needed now was for him to consolidate his position as friend and confidant. He crossed over to Araminta who was still holding a shocked Phyllida.

'I think you and I should help Godmama to her room,' he said. 'Will you call her maid?'

'Yes, yes, of course,' replied Araminta.

Antony went over to Mrs Osborne. 'Come, Godmama,' he said, 'let me help you to your room. Araminta is ringing for your maid.'

'Thank you, Antony.' For once Mrs Osborne was beyond words.

Mrs Quentin looked at her husband over Phyllida's bowed head. 'I'll take her upstairs and see her to her bed,' she said. 'She'll feel better for a sleep I have no doubt.'

Major Quentin sighed. 'Poor girl. Gainford always was a scamp, but I thought him at least an honourable one.'

Mrs Quentin shook her head and, one arm around Phyllida, helped her from the room.

*   *   *

Hereward had stormed out of the house with no very clear idea of what he was going to do beyond a strong desire to throttle Emma. However, the cool night air sobered him and he

201

stopped under a tree to reconsider his position. His first impulse had been to hail a cab and confront Emma at once, but this had several drawbacks. For one thing he was in full evening dress and for another he did not have the money on him. The second proved decisive: he walked back to St James's Square.

The butler opened the door.

'I want Gregg—at once.'

The butler stared at him. 'Now, my lord?'

'Yes, now. I know he's probably asleep, but that can't be helped. I want the phaeton round as soon as possible.'

'Very good, my lord.'

Some twenty minutes later, Hereward, changed into his usual driving clothes with a thick caped driving coat, went down into the hall. Gregg was there waiting.

'The phaeton is outside, my lord.'

'Thank you.'

'What time shall you be back, my lord?'

'I don't know. I'll drive round to the mews and knock you up.'

Hereward climbed up, took the reins and vanished into the darkness leaving his groom scratching his head.

It was past two o'clock when Emma heard the peremptory banging at the door. She climbed out of bed, opened a window and peered out.

'Who is it?'

'Emma! Let me in at once!'

'Good God, Hereward! Whatever is the matter?'

'Never mind that. Just let me in.'

'Well,' said Emma, when they were both upstairs in her bedroom. 'A fine time to come calling, I must say.' She looked at him provocatively through her lashes.

'I've come to restore a piece of your property.' Hereward tossed the licence down on to the bed.

Emma picked it up slowly. 'Where had you this?'

'Lady Selina Lemmon used it this evening in a not very subtle attempt to destroy Phyllida Gainford's good name.'

Emma's mind was racing. Antony? Who else? Though how had Lady Selina acquired it?

'As you very well know,' he added savagely.

'I did not!' The bastard, thought Emma. He must have picked the lock.

'You cannot expect me to believe that!'

'Believe me or not as you will,' Emma shrugged, 'but this is not of my making.'

'You are asking me to believe that this licence came into the hands of Lady Selina by magic?'

'No,' said Emma resignedly, 'probably by Antony Herriot.'

'Antony Herriot? Ah, I see.'

'You haven't been here much, have you? What did you expect me to do? Take up tatting?'

'But I don't understand. What possible advantage could this be to Herriot?'

'Antony wants to lay his hands on Miss Stukeley's money. Mrs Gainford was in the way.'

'So you told him that she wasn't Mrs Gainford at all, because *you* were.'

'No, I did not! Why should I want to do such a thing? Besides, the Gainfords give me an allowance on the strict understanding that the marriage is kept private. What possible advantage could it be to me to tell?'

'But you didn't think to tell me of this marriage?'

'Why should I? It all happened so long ago and I didn't see that it was any of your business.'

'None of my business when you and Gainford were spending all poor Johnny's money?'

'Johnny? Johnny Taunton, you mean? So what? Ambrose won that fairly. Why shouldn't he spend it—with his lawful wife? We got a lot of fun out of it.'

'You ... You.' Words failed Hereward. He had accused Phyllida of living off blood-money and all the time it had been Emma! Emma who had rioted it away with Gainford in the pleasure houses of Brighton. He felt quite sick with rage. And Emma did not even care!

'What is it to do with you?' demanded

204

Emma. 'Why shouldn't I have married Ambrose if I wanted to? When we parted he was in debt and I had the chance to go into the theatre: the settlement suited us both. It's hardly my fault if he committed a bigamous marriage!'

'Your sense of justice did not lead you to stop the wedding?'

'I could never afford a sense of justice,' retorted Emma. 'Only the nobs can afford that. It's a luxury where I come from, Hereward. I didn't begrudge Ambrose his *chère amie*, why should I spoil his fun? There have been times when I've been glad of the paltry two hundred a year I get from the Gainfords, I can tell you.'

'You are going to be needing it! We're through, Emma.'

'Are you going to turn me out of the house now?' asked Emma lightly. 'In my night-dress.'

'No, of course not.' Hereward took an agitated turn around the room, trying to still his chaotic thoughts. He saw again Johnny's body swinging over the stairwell, saw Emma and Gainford laughing, mounds of golden guineas in their hands. God, what was the matter with him? Sir Marmaduke was right: Johnny had been weak, and a traitor to boot. Why visit that on Emma's head? And why did he feel so much disgust at the thought of both Emma and Phyllida having been involved with Ambrose Gainford?

'You can have this house, Emma,' he said at

last. 'The lease is good for another three and a half years or thereabouts, and I'll pay the servants until the end of the year.'

He had meant to be conciliatory, but Emma's temper snapped.

'I see. So you're discarding me? Just like that!' She clicked her fingers. 'What are you going to do now? Perhaps you'd like a try at the second Mrs Ambrose Gainford? Ambrose was very experienced between the sheets. I'm sure he'll have trained the lady to your satisfaction.'

'How dare you!'

'Oh, I can see what's going on under my nose! You want that red-headed creature, so now you're making an excuse to get rid of me. Something that can be twisted round to being *my* fault? Well, if it was my fault to marry Ambrose Gainford, then it was her fault too! And another thing, your precious Johnny was a spy! He tried to worm his way into my bed too; I daresay he thought I might hear something from Ambrose he could sell.'

Emma had hit two nails on the head with such devastating accuracy that Hereward could find no reply.

'I don't know what you're talking about, Emma.'

'I think you do! Now, just go away, Hereward. Get out! I've had enough of being lectured for one night.'

'Very well then.' Hereward took his hat from the chair and put it on. 'Goodbye, Emma. My solicitor will be in touch.'

Emma turned away and did not answer. When he had gone she dashed away a tear or two angrily. So much for marriage into the aristocracy—but perhaps in her heart of hearts she was not too sorry. She was beginning to get bored and restless anyway. Picking up the licence, she threw her dressing-gown over her shoulders and went down to the drawing-room. The floorboards were cold against her bare feet. She crossed to the escritoire and opened the little drawer. There lay Dick's letter. Emma picked it up with a surge of anticipation.

She would sell the lease of the house, get rid of the servants, except perhaps Polly. What did Miss Emma Winter, star of the new Coburg Theatre, want with a house in Chelsea? She would take some rooms, nice ones, near the theatre. Her bedroom would be in pink silk, her drawing-room in the latest Egyptian fashion *and* she could come home at any hour she pleased and bring anybody she fancied with her!

Who wanted a husband anyway?

CHAPTER EIGHT

If Araminta, with the carelessness of youth, had slept soundly through the night, her cousin had not. Phyllida awoke the following morning heavy-eyed and depressed. She remembered the events of the previous evening only spasmodically; Lady Selina's triumphant malice, the warm clasp of Araminta's fingers in her cold ones, Major Quentin's calm voice. But it was Hereward's behaviour which caused her the most anguish. True, he had held Mrs Gainford up to scorn, but he had had not one word for *her*, only an icy look! Thorold had said a few comforting words to her before he left with Lady Gifford, but from Hereward nothing! He had just stormed out in pursuit of Emma Winter.

At nine o'clock the maid came in with some tea. 'Good morning, madam.' She looked at Phyllida sympathetically. Rumours had run round the kitchen quarters like wildfire and Fanny was intensely curious to see if Phyllida had changed somehow now that her married status had gone.

'Oh, tea,' said Phyllida wearily, pulling herself up. 'Is Mrs Osborne awake yet, Fanny?'

'Yes madam. But she says she's not to be disturbed. Had a bad night her maid says.' She paused hopefully, but Phyllida said nothing. 'Ooo, and I nearly forgot, madam. A letter was delivered for you.'

Phyllida pulled her shawl more closely around her and took the letter gingerly. The handwriting was unfamiliar. 'Thank you, Fanny. That will be all.' She broke the seal and

208

spread out the page. It was short and to the point.

If Mrs Ambrose Gainford would like to call on Miss Emma Winter this morning, she might learn something.

There was a card enclosed with Emma's address engraved in an elaborate flowing script.

Phyllida stared at this letter, her mind seething with conjecture. Had Lord Hereward visited Emma last night, and, if so, what had been said? Probably she had persuaded him to disregard it. Even now he might be lying in her arms, convinced that either it wasn't true, or that, even if it was, it did not concern them.

But in her heart of hearts Phyllida knew that it had been as Lady Selina had said. All sorts of little things confirmed it: Ambrose's strange reluctance to write to his parents after the wedding, Mrs Gainford's own attitude, Amelia Heywood's half-warnings. Phyllida now saw, with a numbed and aching heart, that Ambrose might not have murdered Johnny Taunton, but he had been quite capable of betraying the trust of an innocent girl who had been too in love and too naïve to subject his proposals to the thorough investigation they needed.

But whatever had Emma Winter got to say to her?

(Half an hour later Antony, wrapped in an anonymous grey cloak, watched as Phyllida slipped out of the side door and hailed a hackney carriage.)

Back up in Phyllida's room Fanny, who had come to collect the tea tray, found Emma's letter on the floor. She picked it up and scrutinized it regretfully, for she couldn't read.

Phyllida reached the house in Cheyne Row some thirty minutes later and sent up her card. That something had been going on was obvious the moment she stepped through the door. Most of the shutters were still up and the maid who opened the door had been crying, for every now and then she wiped her eyes with the corner of the apron as she showed Phyllida into the drawing-room and hastily opened the curtains.

Phyllida sat down and looked around. Everything bespoke the taste and affluence of the owner: the silk-covered *chaise-longue*, the Persian carpet in muted pinks and golds, the rosewood escritoire. Lord Hereward must be at home here, she thought sadly. Such a lovely room and with a view out over the Thames. He must love Emma Winter very much. It was a thought too painful to bear, she should never have come.

Time passed and though Phyllida could hear movement and voices upstairs nobody came down. She looked at the clock on the mantelpiece, nearly half an hour! She could not stay much longer or her grandmother might be worried. (Had she known Emma she would

210

have realized that she always kept suppliants waiting at least half an hour.) Phyllida was just wondering what to do, whether to summon the maid, or leave a note when the door opened and Polly entered.

'Miss Winter asks what is your business, madam.'

'My business!' echoed Phyllida. 'But I received a letter from Miss Winter this morning asking me to call. Here is the card she sent me.'

Polly took it. 'If you'll excuse me, madam, I'll take it up to her.'

Another ten minutes passed then Polly returned. 'Miss Winter says she never wrote to you, madam. And she'd be obliged if you'd leave. She has nothing to say to you.'

Phyllida flushed scarlet. 'But ... but why?' she stammered.

'I'm sure I can't say, madam,' replied Polly with a sniff. As well as every other servant in the house she had heard Lord Hereward's arrival in the small hours and indeed, by pressing her ear to the keyhole had heard most of the subsequent quarrel. This Mrs Carrots was plainly the cause of the rupture between Hereward and Emma, and what had she got that her mistress hadn't? 'Lord Hereward is nuts about my mistress, madam,' she hissed, 'and I'll thank you not to come poking your nose into what don't concern you!' That'll show her, the uppity madam.

She went to the door and beckoned to the snivelling maid. 'Show this lady out, Nancy,' she said, and with an angry glance at Phyllida, Polly left the room.

Phyllida rose and began to fumble with her gloves.

Nancy looked at Phyllida; she had heard Polly and Emma talking upstairs, Emma laughing at the thought of being able to score off Phyllida. Horrid pigs, she thought, they haven't got a week's wages between them and starvation. She curtseyed to Phyllida.

'Please, mum, excuse the liberty, but I think it was the other gentleman what wrote, pretending to be Miss Winter, like.'

'You mean Lord Hereward?'

'Oh no, mum, not him. He's a nice gentleman, he is. The *other* one, mum. Mr Herriot.'

Phyllida sat down suddenly. 'Mr Herriot!' A horrible suspicion had begun to form in her brain.

'Yes, mum,' said Nancy, pleased with the effect of her announcement. '*She,*' with a jerk of the head upstairs, 'has been seeing Mr Herriot as well. A shifty piece of work in my opinion, mum. Oh, he acts very sweet on *her*, but us servant girls is beneath his notice. Not like his lordship. It's a crying shame.'

To have Lord Hereward and *then* to dally with Antony Herriot! was Phyllida's first coherent thought. She must be mad.

Nancy lowered her voice. 'His lordship comes round last night, mum. Such a banging at the door as you never heard. Why the whole house could hear it. And he says to her...'

'Nancy!' It was Polly's voice. 'Miss wants to know where's her coffee?'

'I'm sorry, mum. Lady Muck calls. I'm afraid I'll have to show you out.'

'Yes, I must go.' Phyllida pushed away the tantalizing possibilities of what Hereward might have said and brought her mind back abruptly to Nancy's other information. There was not a moment to lose. If Nancy was right and it was Mr Herriot who had written the letter, then he could only have wanted her out of the way. Now why? Araminta! He must be planning ... She must return home as quickly as possible.

* * *

'Impossible, Hetty,' said Mrs Osborne sternly. 'They cannot *both* have vanished!'

'No, madam,' replied Hetty obediently.

'I expect they have slipped out for a little early shopping. It is too absurd! Any minute they will be back and you will wonder how you came to be so stupid.'

'Yes, madam.'

'Ask downstairs, Hetty. And apprise me at once if anybody has any information.'

Mrs Osborne had spent the wakeful watches

213

of the night pursuing thoughts of boiling Lady Selina in oil—slowly—incarcerating her in a vampire-ridden cell, throwing her to the lions in some Roman amphitheatre and had finally settled on ostracizing her. How dared she do it? Especially after she, Cecilia Osborne, had overcome her reluctance and condescended to invite her to the ball in the first place. If there was one thing she could not tolerate it was ingratitude. Lady Selina would very soon regret her impertinence.

This morning she would write to her lawyer instructing him to ascertain the truth behind Lady Selina's claim. If it was true, then Phyllida would just have to learn to hold her head up for a few weeks. As for Augusta Gainford, if that lady was wise she would already have started her packing. But how had Lady Selina acquired the marriage certificate?

And where were Phyllida and Araminta?

Mrs Osborne sat bolt upright in her ebony-backed chair, not allowing her back the luxury of resting against a cushion and tried to quell her agitated thoughts. She had never found actions not of her own ordering acceptable, and there had been far too many of them recently. The unexpected arrival of Lord Hereward, therefore, disturbed her still further.

'To what do I owe this visit?' she enquired at her most majestic. If Lady Gifford had sent her grandson to inform her that any hope of a

214

marriage between poor Phyllida and Lord Gifford was at an end, she did not think that she could bear it. She felt old suddenly, old and tired.

'I am come to enquire after Mrs Gainford, and, if you will not think me impertinent, to offer her my support. What Lady Selina said was quite inexcusable!'

'An odious woman,' agreed Mrs Osborne. Then she stopped, hearing a noise on the stairs and wondering if by any miracle it were Araminta or Phyllida. 'Excuse me a moment, my lord.' She rose stiffly and walked to the door. 'Araminta! Phyllida!' she called. 'Is that you!'

'Is anything amiss, ma'am?'

'Neither of my granddaughters appear to be in the house.'

'You think something's happened to them?'

'Certainly not! The very idea is ridiculous!' Mrs Osborne did not approve of unpleasant surprises and usually, when confronted by her icy stare, they slunk away.

There was a scratch at the door. 'Excuse me, madam. I thought you'd like to know.'

'Yes, Hetty. What is it?'

'Mrs Gainford received a letter this morning and then she went out. Least her cloak's not in her wardrobe. I took the liberty of bringing the letter down to you.'

Mrs Osborne took one look at the letter then handed it to Hereward.

'Your arrival is fortunate, my lord. You may be able to throw some light on this.'

'Certainly,' said Hereward dryly, having scanned the letter. 'This letter is not from Emma.'

'*Not* from Miss Winter?'

'No.'

Mrs Osborne picked up her lorgnette and held her hand out again for the letter. This time she recognized the writing: she had had a very pretty letter from the author only a few days before. 'You are right. It is from Antony Herriot.'

'Ah!' Hereward's eyes grew thoughtful. 'I begin to see. Miss Stukeley is a considerable heiress, is she not? There is no time to be lost if I am to catch up with them.'

'Who?'

'Don't worry, madam. I'll bring Miss Stukeley back safe and sound. I haven't yet met the horses that can match my bays.'

'But where are you going?'

'The road to Gloucestershire, where else? Look to Mr Herriot, ma'am, if you want the villain. I'll see myself out.' He picked up his gloves and hat and left. She could hear him running down the stairs and he was gone.

*　　*　　*

Antony had watched as Phyllida left the house on her precipitate visit to Emma and, having

216

seen the cab disappear, turned back to his companion. 'Right, Joe. You know what to do as soon as I fetch the lady?'

'Head straight for the Gloucester road and never mind a bit 'o screeching 'cos the lady's having the vapours,' he said with a leer, wiping his nose with the back of his hand.

'Good. Mind you don't forget.'

The front door to Mrs Osborne's house was open, but a maid was there, cleaning the steps. Antony watched her for a few moments, his busy mind wondering how he was to get in without being seen. Araminta was in the breakfast-room, he had seen her pass briefly in front of the window some ten minutes ago. He doubted whether Mrs Osborne would be up after so exhausting an evening. The chances were that Araminta would be alone—and Antony always had believed in his luck.

The devil was with him this morning, for a gypsy woman, with two scrawny brats, came up to the house, and in shooing them away energetically with broom and tongue, the maid left her door unguarded for a moment and Antony slipped inside.

Araminta was, as he had hoped, alone in the breakfast-room.

'Antony! Whatever are you doing here?'

'I was let in. Didn't you hear my knock?'

'No, I must have been thinking of someone—I mean something else.' Araminta blushed at her mistake, but Antony did

217

not notice.

'Araminta, have you seen your cousin this morning?'

'Phyl?' Araminta's eyes widened in sudden alarm. 'No.'

'I've just seen her at the Golden Cross Inn.'

'Oh no! You think she's gone home?'

Antony sighed heavily, 'I fear so. I was just too late to prevent her. By the time I recollected myself the coach had gone. I enquired, of course, and they confirmed that a red-haired lady had boarded the Gloucestershire coach.'

'Oh, poor Phyl! Whatever shall we do?'

'I could go after her,' said Antony doubtfully, 'only I doubt that she'd listen to me.'

'*I* could come with you!'

'Good heavens, no!'

'Whyever not?' demanded Araminta.

'What would people say?' asked Antony, adding a little fuel to the fire.

'What do I care what people say? It's Phyl I'm concerned about.'

'I'm not sure...'

'Well, I am.'

'I don't think that Godmama would approve at all!'

'She won't know!' cried Araminta triumphantly. 'Now, no more arguing, Antony. My mind is made up. I'll just go and fetch a cloak.'

Thorold, thought Araminta, as she reached

218

her room and began to pull things out of her wardrobe in her impatience to find her cloak. Thorold was coming at eleven! Whatever should she do? Surely he would understand how important it was to bring Phyllida back? Her running away would be fatal! Look at Lady Bessborough and the Countess of Oxford! They had both had countless affairs and they were accepted. Why should Phyllida not be accepted when her false marriage was not even her fault?

She would write to Thorold explaining, and somebody could deliver it.

She met Fanny on the stairs on the way down.

'Please, miss,' said Fanny. 'It's Mrs Gainford. She went out early this morning, miss, and she's not back yet. I don't want to worry Mrs Osborne with it.'

'I should think not!' said Araminta with a sympathetic shudder, for doubtless poor Fanny would be subjected to an angry tirade. 'Don't worry, I know all about it and I'm going after her!'

It must be admitted that amid her concern for her cousin, part of Araminta relished the secret escapade. And this time it was for real!

'Oh, miss! You are brave!'

Araminta's eyes sparkled. 'Perhaps I shall meet with a highwayman, Fanny!'

'Don't say such things, miss.'

'Now never mind. I shall be quite safe, I

assure you. I want you to deliver this note to Lord Gifford, Fanny. At once. It's most important.'

'Very good, miss.'

'And not a *word* to anybody, especially not Mrs Osborne!'

'Wild horses wouldn't drag it from me, miss.'

Wild horses, thought Araminta with a shudder, then pushed it aside. Phyllida was more important than her vague uneasiness. She ran downstairs to the breakfast-room.

'I'm ready, Antony. Come, let us go. We have not a moment to lose.'

The street was quiet outside as Araminta and Antony slipped out of the side door, with only a few housemaids cleaning the steps or polishing the brass door handles. They turned the corner and Antony gestured silently to the waiting carriage. If it had crossed Araminta's mind that this was a repetition of a similar journey with Antony once before, she might have hesitated, but her mind was too full of Phyllida and Thorold to have any time for consideration of the dangers of her own position.

Antony ushered her into the carriage, climbed in after her and closed the door on both of them, with no protest whatsoever from his intended victim.

*   *   *

220

Lady Gifford couldn't make Thorold out at all that morning. Usually he ate his breakfast silently and in haste, his mind obviously elsewhere. If she wanted a question answered she had to ask it several times in a loud voice as often as not, before he descended from whatever rarefied intellectual plane he was inhabiting to a more commonplace region where she could reach him. Today, however, he seemed relaxed and cheerful, even asking her how she'd slept and whether he could pour her any more coffee.

It had been Hereward who was preoccupied and silent, vouchsafing her questions only a brief 'yes' or 'no'. He had stared at his coffee for perhaps ten minutes, crumbled his toast and then pushed both away impatiently and left the room.

Thorold had not stayed long after Hereward.

'I shall be out this morning, Grandmama,' he said, happily. 'I hope I may have some good news for you at luncheon.'

'Gracious me! What sort of good news, pray?'

'That must wait,' replied Thorold and left the room.

He thus missed, by five minutes, the arrival of Araminta's letter.

He went first to have his hair cut and then, after a few moments' hesitation, turned towards South Audley Street and Tessiers.

Unlike Hereward, who had frequently visited Tessiers for fans, posy holders and other trifles that gentlemen might wish to offer ladies, Thorold rarely visited a jeweller. He had had the family jewellery reset for Drusilla, but Lady Gifford had overseen that operation. The last time he had visited a jeweller was probably some two or three years previously to choose a snuff box for an elderly uncle's seventieth birthday.

It was with some diffidence that he entered the shop. Hereward, of course, was well known, but nobody recognized Thorold and he was left with the doorman regarding him suspiciously as the assistants attended to more important customers.

'May I help you, sir?' he was asked at last.

'I'm not sure what to buy,' said Thorold looking around him helplessly.

'Who might it be for,' the assistant enquired patiently. 'Your mother perhaps? Your wife?'

'No! No! A young lady. Very young.'

'Ah, a Christening present.'

'No, she's about eighteen. I want something special, but something that she may accept.'

'I see.' The assistant had the picture now. The gentleman in front of him was in love. And lovers could be persuaded to buy the most expensive trifles. He became most attentive.

'Jewellery, I'm afraid sir, is out. No young lady would be allowed to accept jewellery— unless, of course, you have the felicity to be

222

engaged to the young lady? No? Ah well, sir, we must hope!

'If you will step this way, sir, I will show you a number of little objects that must always be acceptable.' He lifted out some velvet-lined drawers and laid them on the table. 'An exquisite little trinket box, perhaps? This one here is French, Sèvres, of the last century. Or we have some ladies' opera glasses—these are gold, decorated in dark-blue enamel with seed pearls.'

'I'm not sure...' began Thorold

'Or a fan? This one is hand-painted, "Nymphs assisting at the toilette of Venus".' The assistant looked at Thorold's face and added hastily, 'Or a handsome prayer book cover in the finest leather with your lady's initials in gold?'

* * *

While Thorold was pondering on the Sèvres trinket box, Araminta was beginning to feel uncomfortable. Her first anxiety had carried her past the Tyburn turnpike and out towards the Western Road. She had sat bolt upright on the edge of her seat as if expecting to see the Gloucester stage coach at any minute, though she knew it must be at least an hour ahead, possibly more.

The carriage they were in, a two-seater only, had plainly seen better days: the varnish was cracked and peeling and the springs uncomfortable. The windows too were dirty so that she could hardly see out and had to rub at the pane with the corner of her handkerchief.

'Oxford—48 miles' read a signpost.

At least they were on the right road. Araminta couldn't help feeling a little uneasy, but surely everything was all right?

'The horses seem very slow,' she ventured after some moments' silence.

'They're all right.'

'Are you sure we'll catch them up soon?'

'Yes, now be quiet, Araminta.'

Araminta sank back against the squabs and tried to quell her growing feeling that something was wrong.

* * *

Phyllida arrived home shortly before eleven, her arrival almost simultaneous with Thorold's. His carriage, with his crest on the panels and drawn by four glossy chestnuts, trotted smartly round the corner and pulled up outside the house just as Phyllida had finished paying off her cab. The coachman went to the horses' heads and Thorold jumped down.

'Mrs Gainford! You here!'

'Yes?'

'Good God, something is very wrong! I went out early this morning and didn't get home till about twenty minutes ago. I have only just received a note from Araminta saying that she had gone with Mr Herriot after you. Towards Gloucester.'

'I feared as much!' cried Phyllida. 'Come in, Lord Gifford. We'd better tell Grandmama.'

They found Mrs Osborne, her face strained and white, sitting in the drawing-room, staring unseeing at the wall. She started as Phyllida and Thorold came in.

'Thank God! Phyllida!'

'We have something to tell you, Grandmama.'

'I think I know it. My godson has abducted Araminta.'

'How do you know, Grandmama?'

'Lord Hereward has been here. Hetty found your letter from Emma Winter and between us we realized that a letter in Antony's writing sending you out of the way could only mean that Antony had designs on Araminta.'

'Fortunately Miss Stukeley wrote to me,' Thorold broke in. 'She is gone after the Gloucester stage coach, so she thinks, with Mr Herriot.'

'So Lord Hereward surmised. He left about twenty minutes ago. I confess it took me longer to arrive at the same conclusion.' She smiled a little grimly at Phyllida. 'I must be getting old.'

'The Western Road. I should like you to come with me, Mrs Gainford,' said Thorold, turning towards the door.

'Of course.'

'*You* are going as well? What use will that be, pray? And why, may I ask, is my granddaughter committing the gross indiscretion of writing to an unattached male?'

'I need Mrs Gainford to chaperone Araminta,' replied Thorold firmly. 'Hereward, I take it, has gone in his phaeton. You will hardly wish your granddaughter to arrive back in an open carriage—the butt for every gossip in Town?

'As for my being unattached, that is no longer true. My heart has been Araminta's for some time. And now, if you will excuse us ma'am, we must be off.'

'*Araminta's!*' echoed Mrs Osborne. But they had gone.

* * *

Araminta stared out of the grimy window and tried not to wonder whether she would ever see her home or Thorold again. Several times Antony had poked his head out of the window. He had said it was to see if the stage coach was in sight, but it looked to Araminta's uneasy mind as if he were looking behind not ahead. Did he fear pursuit? She was beginning to feel queasy too from the jolting of the wheels, and the stuffiness of the dusty interior was giving her a headache. When, after a particularly severe lurch the carriage stopped, Araminta could only feel relieved.

226

'Sorry, Guv.' The coachman's face peered in at the window. ''orse thrown a shoe.' He leered at Araminta, showing a row of broken teeth. He smelt too, a mixture of dirt and drink, and Araminta shrank back, pulling her cloak more closely around her. Antony opened the door and jumped out. Araminta rapidly surveyed her position.

Why, oh why, had she not listened to Phyllida earlier? She could not now conceal from herself that Antony was up to no good. He had employed that horrid man, he had insisted that she did not inform her grandmother, and since she had entered the carriage his attitude had changed. No longer solicitious and obliging, he was now curt and off-hand.

What did he want? Was it, as Phyl had suggested, her fortune? Was that it? An honest man would rather have come properly to her grandmother to ask for her hand, however romantic the idea of a runaway match might seem. What was he planning?

Araminta now doubted whether Phyllida was on the stage coach at all. Maybe he had managed to get her out of the house for a while to lend credence to his story and ensure that she, Araminta, would be alone.

In her hat was a long hat-pin. Araminta removed it and pinned it carefully inside the sash of her dress. There! She'd show him if he tried anything!

Antony opened the door. 'We're taking the side road to Denham,' he said. 'We passed it about twenty-five yards back. They'll have a blacksmith there.'

'May I get out?' asked Araminta pathetically. 'I do feel so sick.'

'Very well, but only while Joe turns the carriage.'

Araminta hopped out and looked around. If she ran Antony would be sure to catch her. The road was clear both ways, there was nowhere that she could hide. In any case, what would she do twenty miles from London with no money?

At least she had had the sense to write to Thorold. Surely he would set off after her—perhaps Phyllida had even arrived back home by now.

'I just need to retire behind the tree,' she said. 'I shan't be a minute.'

'Very well,' said Antony curtly, 'I'll be with the carriage.' The carriage was now pointing towards Denham.

She had a couple of minutes. Think, Araminta, think! There was an oak tree above her. Swiftly she pulled off her hat and, looking to see that Antony's back was turned, tossed it up into the tree, where it hung some twelve feet up, its yellow ribbons fluttering in the breeze. Then she made her way back to the waiting carriage.

It would mark her whereabouts. With a bit

of luck no passing ploughboy would retrieve it, and it was unlikely that Antony would notice its absence. She might have been exceptionally stupid, but at least now she had done something sensible!

Denham proved to be a small village boasting only one inn, the Cross Keys, a ramshackle, tumbledown affair with several sheds at the side and a number of pigs and hens rooting about in the yard.

Araminta stared at it aghast. 'But it's dreadful!' she cried.

Antony laughed. 'Couldn't be better,' he said in an aside to Joe that was just audible, 'Nobody would think of looking for her here!'

*   *   *

Phyllida sank back in Thorold's carriage and closed her eyes. She could not get Polly's venomous voice out of her head, 'Lord Hereward is nuts about my mistress'. Perhaps it was true, she thought wearily. Perhaps all the time he was only being kind because he was sorry for her. Now he knew the true story he had returned to Emma, thankful to be rid of so embarrassing an acquaintance.

When she and Thorold caught him up she would not betray by so much as a flicker that she had ever felt anything for him: she would not court humiliation by looking to him for anything other than the most

229

commonplace courtesies.

*　　*　　*

After leaving Mrs Osborne's Hereward had paused only to collect his pistols and some money from St James's Square before setting off at a brisk trot towards the Tyburn Turnpike. Reviewing what he knew, he tried to forecast Antony's movements.

From what Emma had let fall, it was undoubtedly Herriot who had stolen her marriage certificate, even if Lady Selina was the person to use it. It was Herriot who had written to Phyllida sending her off on a false trail to Emma's. These facts could not possibly be unconnected with Miss Stukeley's disappearance.

Now, where would he take her? The pretext, Hereward guessed, had probably been Phyllida's supposed flight home. Would Herriot have taken the Western Road, at least at first, to lull Araminta's suspicions? Or would he have headed north towards Gretna Green? After some reflection, Hereward rejected the Gretna idea. Herriot would not have had the money necessary for so long a journey, and besides, to drag a reluctant bride 300 miles to the border would be foolhardy to say the least.

No, Herriot's most likely course of action would be to head west and at some conveniently remote spot contrive some minor accident to the carriage or horses which would necessitate Araminta spending the night in his company.

What would they be travelling in? A two-seater, probably. Closed, of course, with two or even only one horse. Hired. Undoubtedly shabby. Probably with some sort of coachman, otherwise Araminta, being a young lady of spirit, might escape unseen from the carriage. He would enquire after such a vehicle at the turnpike.

Hereward was in luck. Aye, said the turnpike keeper, just such a carriage had passed about half an hour ago. No, he didn't see a lady, but he'd heard one talking. He'd remembered it because it seemed odd that so well-spoken a young lady should be in so rackety a carriage.

Hereward described Antony as well as he could.

'That's 'im, sir. And the bloke what drove the 'orses is a villainous-looking geezer with a crammed-down felt 'at like, and 'is teeth black and broken like a lot o' chipped tombstones.'

Hereward thanked him, tossed him half a guinea and was off. At Northolt he enquired again. Yes, such a carriage had passed through some twenty minutes previously.

It was some ten minutes later that he saw the hat.

Now Hereward had not been supporting elegant and expensive mistresses for years for nothing: he knew a modiste's creation when he saw it—even twelve foot up an oak tree. He couldn't swear that it was Araminta's, of course, but it was undoubtedly the hat of a young lady of fashion.

He pulled up his horses, jumped down and went to examine the tracks. Something, a light carriage, had turned here recently. Ah, one of the horses had cast a shoe: here was the imprint of a bare hoof in the dirt.

He went back to his team, turned them and followed the tracks in front of him. Ah, a signpost and yes! the carriage had gone left. Denham, it read, half a mile. Should he follow his intuition and take it, or should he continue westward?

* * *

'Well, sir,' demanded Araminta, her diminutive figure stiff with outrage, 'what have you got to say for yourself? Why have you locked me in this horrid room for twenty minutes?'

'So that you would not run away, my sweet,' replied Antony, coming towards her and flicking the door shut with one careless hand.

'What of Phyllida, pray. Is *her* plight of no concern to you?'

'None at all,' replied Antony coolly.

'May I ask if she ever was on this stage coach?'

'The Gloucester stage coach doesn't leave London until the evening.'

'I see.' Araminta surveyed the room quickly. Small, beer-smelling, dirty, it had but one door and that Antony was standing in front of. The window opened out on to the yard, but the panes were small and leaded and, judging by the spiders' webs, it had not been opened for years.

Supposing she got free, would the landlord's wife befriend her? Thinking of that sour and greedy countenance, Araminta doubted it. Would Joe take her back to London on the promise of a handsome reward? That, too, seemed unlikely, she had heard him several times shouting for more ale from the taproom underneath.

'No,' said Antony, reading her thoughts. 'The landlord would want to see ready gold and you don't have your purse with you, do you? As for Joe, he's a man who likes a go at the women. I really don't think you'd be advised to trust yourself to him—even if he were sober, which I doubt.'

'W ... what do you want?' Araminta's voice trembled slightly, the chance of rescue now seemed very far away. How *stupid* she had been! How unbelievably naïve.

'Your fortune, Araminta. We shall be married the moment we return to London.'

'No!'

'Oh yes! We shall spend the night together,

in this rustic retreat, and by the morning, I assure you, you will be only too glad to consent to any terms I care to offer.'

'I won't!'

'We'll see.' Antony took a step towards her.

'Don't come near me!' Araminta felt for her hat-pin, its steely point was reassuringly sharp.

Antony came closer. 'Don't be silly. You'll enjoy it. You were quite an eager little thing in Mudie's Library, I seem to recall.'

'How could you, Antony!' Araminta's eyes were brimming. 'After all Grandmama has done for you.'

'She's a bossy old hag!' said Antony savagely. 'Trying to buy me off with a miserable hundred! I want your money, Araminta. Sickly sentiment has no room in my life.' He had come right up to her now. He raised his hands and with one brutal movement ripped the dress from her shoulders.

Araminta screamed.

There was a noise on the stairs and a peremptory banging at the door. Antony leapt back, one hand going swiftly to his pocket.

'Look out!' shrieked Araminta, as Hereward rushed into the room, 'he has a pistol!'

There was a loud report. Hereward staggered back, one hand clasped to his shoulder.

'You!' gasped Antony, his face white with rage. Lord Hereward, who could pay for so luscious a woman as Emma Winter, who had

234

everything money could buy, had now come after Araminta, doubtless intending to wed her and add her £60,000 to his own immense fortune. Hatred swept over him. He raised his hand again to fire the other barrel. This time he couldn't miss. Hereward was lying stunned against the door post: he could put a bullet through his head at point-blank range.

Araminta rushed forward as he raised the pistol, hitting up his arm as hard as she could. The bullet ricocheted off the ceiling, sending down showers of dust and plaster and buried itself in the wall.

With one savage blow Antony hit Araminta across the room. She fell heavily against the window which, rotted by years of neglect, fell out with a splintering of wood and glass, sending a sudden burst of sunlight into the dust and settling plaster.

'Thorold!' shrieked Araminta, leaning dizzily against the frame, seeing a familiar carriage sweep up. Thorold and Phyllida jumped out. Araminta swung her legs over the window sill and, heedless of her dust-grimed cheeks, bruised ribs and exposed breasts, slid down into the Earl's arms and kissed him as though she could never stop. Then she burst into tears on his shoulder.

'Your brother!' she gasped. 'Antony's shot him!'

Phyllida's heart seemed to stop beating for a full minute. All her resolutions of a polite distance towards Hereward vanished. She picked up her skirts and ran.

When she reached the top of the stairs it was to see Hereward slumped against the wall, blood seeping sluggishly from his shoulder and Antony, his back towards her, busily engaged in reloading his pistol.

Phyllida, after one swift look around, seized a pewter candlestick from the mantelpiece and calmly hit Antony over the head with it with all the force she could muster. For one nerve-racking moment nothing happened, then the pistol dropped and Antony fell to the floor with a thump.

'Well done,' Hereward's voice came weakly from behind her. 'I couldn't have done it better myself.'

Phyllida picked up Antony's pistol and went to kneel beside him.

'Phyllida,' said Hereward weakly, reaching for her hand.

'Hush,' Phyllida blushed, 'are you all right?'

Hereward seemed to have recovered his sense of humour with his wits, for he dragged himself up a little and felt his shoulder gingerly. 'My heart is aching, most dreadfully,' he said plaintively.

'Your heart!' echoed Phyllida alarmed.

'Yes. I should feel a lot better if you'd kiss me.'

'My lord! You are not yourself!'

'Phyllida,' said Hereward in a stronger

voice, 'I felt like murdering Herriot on the way here, for what he'd done to you. Emma told me last night that it was he who stole her marriage lines and somehow induced Lady Selina to use them at the ball.'

'Mr Herriot!'

'Yes. But never mind that. Phyllida, dearest, look at me.'

Colouring, Phyllida did so.

'I love you. Will you do me the very great honour of becoming my wife?'

'M ... me?' stammered Phyllida, trying to quell the rising happiness which threatened to overwhelm her. 'But ... you know about me! I wasn't even married to Ambrose!'

'I don't give a damn about Gainford,' said Hereward, suddenly finding that it was true. 'I want to marry you. The only question is, do you want to marry me?'

'Oh yes! So much!' sighed Phyllida.

Hereward held out his one sound arm. Then, in spite of such minor inconveniences as a bullet in his shoulder and his would-be murderer supine on the floor not two yards away, he covered Phyllida's willing mouth with his own and promptly forgot the world.

When Thorold and Araminta, who was wrapped up in Thorold's cloak, came in some minutes later, both looking slightly bemused and blissfully happy, it was to find Hereward and Phyllida, covered with dust and plaster, locked in a passionate embrace. Antony was lying on the floor, a fallen pewter candlestick beside him.

'Good God!' cried Thorold. 'Whatever's happened to him?'

Hereward raised his head. 'Phyllida knocked him out.'

'Oh, Phyl, you are clever!' cried Araminta admiringly. 'I have been very stupid,' she added with resolution, 'going off with Antony and causing all this trouble. I see that now. Please forgive me, Phyl. And you too, Lord Hereward.'

Phyllida, smiling, held out her hand to her cousin.

'I'm going to marry Thorold,' finished Araminta triumphantly. 'Isn't that wonderful?'

'And Phyllida has consented to become my wife,' said Hereward rising, his sound hand on Phyllida's shoulder for support. He turned and smiled into her eyes.

'I wish you both very happy,' said Araminta solemnly. Then a thought struck her. 'Good heavens, Phyl, I've just realized. I shall be a Countess!'

* * *

The wedding in St George's, Hanover Square, of Lord Hereward FitzIvor to Miss Phyllida Danby, was generally acknowledged to be one of the high spots of the Season. The bride in a wedding dress of old gold silk looked happy and beautiful. The bridegroom (whose mysterious wound had been the object of much romantic speculation) looked serious and handsome. As the bride came up the aisle he turned with such a look of adoration that at least one of the female guests felt quite faint and had to be pinched firmly by her mama.

The chief bridesmaid, Miss Araminta Stukeley, soon to be wed to the Earl of Gifford, was looking ravishingly pretty and little Lady Caroline FitzIvor stole all hearts by insisting on pulling a toy dog on wheels up the aisle behind her.

If Lady Selina Lemmon (who was not invited) was heard to mutter that possibly Miss Danby wanted so public a wedding in case anybody doubted that it had taken place at all, her remarks were dismissed as merely malicious. When, some weeks later, her popularity waning with Phyllida's reinstatement, she took herself off on a prolonged tour of the drearier German spas, her departure was unlamented.

The absence of Mrs Osborne's godson, Antony Herriot, occasioned more speculation. There had been rumours of his involvement in the Danby-Gifford affair, but nobody knew for certain. All that was known was that he had left his rooms, resigned from his club, and his old gambling haunts knew him no more.

Mr Danby, pushed by his strong-minded
239

prospective son-in-law, came up to London for the wedding, and any lingering doubts about Phyllida's respectability were laid to rest. Mr Danby was obviously a gentleman. He settled down in London, happily poring over Thorold's books, treating Mrs Osborne with a sort of abstracted politeness and becoming quite taken with Araminta.

'You have been singularly foolish, Mr Danby,' said Mrs Osborne, as though he was five rather than fifty. 'However, I suppose I must let bygones be bygones. You may count yourself my son-in-law!'

She was even more conciliatory after the wedding, watching Hereward and Phyllida greet their guests for the wedding breakfast: Phyllida happy and relaxed and Hereward looking tenderly at her.

'I was quite put out to learn that Lord Hereward wanted to marry Phyllida,' she admitted to Lady Gifford. 'I had planned for her to marry Lord Gifford. But, do you know, I think this might work out very well, very well indeed!'

We hope you have enjoyed this Large Print book. Other Chivers Press or Thorndike Press Large Print books are available at your library or directly from the publishers. For more information about current and forthcoming titles, please call or write, without obligation, to:

Chivers Press Limited
Windsor Bridge Road
Bath BA2 3AX
England
Tel. (01225) 335336

OR

Thorndike Press
P.O. Box 159
Thorndike, Maine 04986
USA
Tel. (800) 223–6121 (U.S. & Canada)
In Maine call collect: (207) 948–2962

All our Large Print titles are designed for easy reading, and all our books are made to last.